Filthy Forbidden Erotic Sex Stories:

Adults Erotica Collection- BDSM, Daddy Domination, Gangbangs, Hot Wives, Anal, Bi-Sexual Threesomes, Foot Fetish, Role-Play, MILFs & More

Written By:

G.G. Goode

Goode Publications

Contents

The Cuffed Prisoner

Chained Up BDSM

I didn't really know how I got here.

The last thing I remembered were all of the people coming into the bar, asking for me. I said I was her, and then, with just one touch, I was knocked the fuck out.

But here I was, a prisoner in a strange place. I looked around, shackled, realizing the state that I was in.

"What's going on here?" I asked out loud.

I noticed that I was alone. The dark, dreary place had no signs of others. I almost wondered if this was some sort of dungeon. But then, I heard the door open up ahead, and the sound of footsteps.

I tried to gauge if there was someone else here, but it didn't seem like there was. I was all alone.

I also noticed my clothes were torn asunder. What did these people do to me? I knew I was wearing a sweater and some pants at the bar, but they were...gone.

So what was I here for?

The footsteps grew closer. I paused, bracing myself as I looked forward. That's when I saw it.

A man. He had blonde hair, piercing green eyes, and a smile that seemed to send shivers down my spine. I don't know if I should be thankful that he's here, or worried shitless about this.

"There you are. You're finally awake," he said to me.

"What are you talking about?" I said.

"Come now, quit playing stupid with me honey. I just wanted to see what you were up to cutie. If there were of course...any big changes in your face, and what was going on," he said.

Was this guy for real? I paused, trying to figure out if I was making the right choice, or the wrong one.

Probably the wrong one.

I tried to move, but the chains were pretty strong, and as I sat there, he looked at me.

"So it's you. The conspirator trying to start a revolution in the kingdom," he said.

Oh, it was definitely that. I realized that he wanted me for treason.

See, I was a revolutionary in the shadows, someone who made sure that I worked for the people, but was never seen. I even went by a different name and made sure to hide everything. That is, until now.

And I realized at this point this man was one of the few royal guardsmen that could royally fuck me up if I'm not careful.

Fuck.

I tried to move, but I was unable to do so. He simply laughed.

"Look at you, pathetic. Man, I told them to disrobe you, but I guess that's not happening. Oh well, I'll work with what I've got," he said.

Work with what he's got? What did he have planned?

I looked at him, unsure as to what he wanted to do at this point, but then he grabbed my chin, looking into my eyes.

"I see. You don't show fear, do you?"

"Why would I?"

"Because you should know by now that little mouth you've got is going to get you into trouble," he said to me.

"So what if it does. It's not like you're going to kill me. You know better than that," I told him.

He looked at me, and then nodded.

"Very true. You are one of the richest people in town, hiding your wealth and pretending to be part of our side. I always despised people like you," he said.

"Well, I wasn't a big fan of you either. So what's it going to be? You going to torture me? Ask me to give that information up? Because I'm sure as shit not doing that," I said.

"No. I have a better use for you," he said.

I paused, trying to figure out what he had in mind. I didn't know what he would do, but then, his face curled into a smile.

"I'm going to make you pay for what you've done. With your body of course," he said.

Hold on...did he just say....

"My...body?" I asked him.

"Did I stutter?" the man said.

I looked up at him, eying his body. I noticed his eyes were glazing over me, and I took a deep breath, enjoying the nature of things. I felt really curious about this, and I was a little bit worried, but there was something pulling me to him, whatever it may be.

"No...you didn't," I said.

"There we go...good girl," he said.

I tried to hold back from moaning as he looked into my eyes. I was supposed to be a revolutionary, someone who didn't take shit from anyone! And yet here I was, my eyes glued to him, enjoying the way his eyes seemed to just look at me completely.

I took a deep breath, enjoying the way things were, and the way his hands reached out, touching the very tip of my shirt. I was a mess, and I knew that if I didn't stop, things would definitely get much more interesting.

His hands moved up towards my neck, holding my head up, looking deep into my eyes. I let out a gasp as he leaned forward, his lips mere inches from me.

"Well, how about we make a little deal?" he asked.

"A...deal?" I asked him.

"Yes. You didn't hear me fucking stutter. If you let me...have my fun with you, I'll let you go. Simple as that you know," he said to me.

I looked at him, seeing the way his eyes met mine. I had a weird feeling about all of this. And yet, I couldn't help but wonder just what else this man had in store for me.

"So you'll let me go?"

"When I'm done, sure," he told me.

I paused, thinking about this.

"Sure, let's do it," I said.

Before I knew it, he moved his hands towards my shirt, grabbing it and pulling it off. My breasts were exposed, causing me to let out a small gasp of surprise.

"Good girl. You know exactly what to do then," he said.

"I'm only giving you this because I know that you'll let me go," I spat.

He then smacked me, causing me to let out a small gasp.

"Don't speak unless you're told to. Got it. If you make too much noise, I won't hesitate to kill you and make it an accident," he muttered.

Shit, I really did need to be careful. I looked at him for a moment, and then nodded.

"Good girl. Now let's see what happens next," he purred.

Soon, he leaned his hands downward, touching my breasts. I struggled to hold back. I wasn't going to lie, this guard, even though he was a bit of an asshole, was kind of hot if I do say so myself.

"You have such a nice body," he purred, touching the tips of my nipples. I struggled to move about, stopped by the feeling of the chains. I let out a small cry, and then he smiled.

"Damn look at you. Already a slut for my touches and I've barely done anything. That's adorable," he purred.

I flushed, looking at him, struggling to say anything to him. I didn't want him to think that I enjoyed this or anything. But his hands felt good, and the little touch against my nipples was enough to make me shiver with delight, and moan slightly. Every single touch was enough to turn me the fuck on, and there was something fun about all of this. He continued to touch my nipples, teasing them with his fingers, rubbing them, and I let out a small cry.

"You're such a needy little slut, already wet as hell. I can see it between your legs. You want my cock, don't you? You can answer," he said to me, teasing my nipple.

I let out another sound, pushing my hips forward, letting out a gasp.

"I'm not...going to give you that satisfaction," I said.

"I see. Well, I guess that means I'm going to have to tease you even more. And I'll make sure that you enjoy it. You're lying right now, and you should be a little bit more open about your feelings. You're open about your feelings regarding the country, and being a traitorous bitch, I'm sure you can be open about how good it feels, right?" he teased.

I flushed, moaning in pleasure. Every single touch, every single motion, it was all...driving me fucking crazy. He then moved his hands downwards, resting against my pussy. He rubbed the edges, making me shiver, but I tried my best to hold back the moans that came with this.

"There we go. Good girl," he said, rubbing me there.

I shivered, letting out a small cry as his hands continued to touch me, moving towards my thighs, cupping them slightly. I let out a small, garbled sound, aching for more from him as I started to feel him move his hand around. Every little touch, even though it wasn't what I was expecting, continued to turn me on. I shivered, crying out loud as he did this.

"You're already losing control, aren't you? Such a good little slut," he said.

He then moved towards my legs, cupping and teasing them and watching me shiver with delight. The little ghosts of touches, the little caresses, it was all just...so fucking good. I ached for it, I needed more, and I knew for a fact that this was definitely getting to the point where even though I'd try not to show my feelings, it was only getting harder and harder to do.

"What's the matter? Struggling to hold back?" he teased.

He moved his hands towards my inner thigh again, touching and caressing them. He was right up against the very entrance of my pussy, and I suddenly felt that need, that desire, and that ache for him.

He then moved his hands towards my pussy, teasing the very tip of it, making me let out a small, choked sound.

"There we go...good girl," he said.

He then rubbed against me, making me shiver with enjoyment as he continued to press into me more and more. Everything was just...so nice. So damn perfect, and I ached for the feeling. I wanted more, and I wanted his touch.

I then noticed his hands move towards me, grabbing my pants. Was he going to pull them off? But no, he simply grabbed the sides, ripping them off my body. He slid them off, pulling them to the chains, and then he ripped them.

I realized he would probably do the same with my panties too. I didn't know what his plans were. But then, he grabbed my panties, throwing them off my body.

"There, now you look perfect," he said.

I shivered, realizing that I both liked this, and didn't like this. Would I get my clothes back? And if I didn't…what did he have planned.

He let his hands rest downward, touching the very tip of my pussy, rubbing the tip of it, and causing me to let out a yelp but I liked the way that it felt.

"You like that?" he said.

"M-maybe I do," I said.

"Come on, we can make this easy, or much harder honey," he said.

His hand dipped inside and started massaging the tender area and I closed my eyes. I was at this man's mercy. Even though it wasn't right, I wanted it, and soon, before I knew it, I tensed up, letting out a small cry, enjoying the feeling.

"Fuck," I breathed out.

"There you go. Good girl," he said.

There was only one thing that I could do. And that of course was to indulge in the pleasure, and the fun that came with this. His hands moved towards me, rubbing the tip of my clit, and I let out a breathy sound.

"Fuck," I said.

"Well, you going to finally let go? Going to finally make those delicious sounds as I tease you?" he said to me.

I shivered. Was I going to let him get the best of me? Maybe, but I didn't want to let that happen.

"Maybe," I said.

"Well, how does a little bit of teasing sound then? Fun huh?" he said.

Fuck I knew I probably should've kept my damn mouth shut. His hands moved outwards, touching the tip of my clit, rubbing it in small circles. I started to close my eyes, moaning in pleasure as I started to hold my body there, enjoying the sensation of this. He wanted me to respond, to react, and I knew he was doing this damn teasing to get the best of me.

He then moved his hands towards my entrance, just barely touching it. I looked into his eyes, seeing the smirk that he had, and I shivered.

He was enjoying this. The motherfucker was teasing me on purpose! I felt like he was getting a thrill from seeing me in an agony of want, clinging to every part of him, letting out a small moan of surprise and need.

"Fuck," I said to him.

"What's the matter dear?" he asked me.

"I'm just…. I'm just trying to hold back," I muttered.

"Why do that? You are clearly enjoying this," he said.

His hands were right there, creating the phantom pain that I enjoyed. I knew that letting go would probably be for the best.

Maybe I needed to do that. I started to close my eyes, realizing that I was already a mess, and that I wanted to just embrace it, and experience more.

That's when I let go. I started closing my eyes, letting out a small hum, feeling good about this. For a moment, I felt his fingers press deep within, making me shiver with delight, crying out loud. I started to hold the area there, pushing my hips up, feeling everything just slowly unwind.

He then started moving within me, pressing his fingers in. The feeling was making me lose my mind, every touch sending me to a whole new plane of existence. And yet, I loved it. I wanted him to do this, and I ached for him, wanting more.

"Fuck," I said, feeling the fingers moving within me become shallower. He was doing this on purpose.

To make me beg. He started dipping them slowly deeper in, and I bit my lip.

"Fuck,' I muttered.

"What's the matter there?" he asked me.

"I'm not…going to give in," I said.

"Whatever you say there dear," he said.

He then continued the torment, the tease.

"I'm…fuck," I said.

"You're what? Go ahead, spit it out. I'm sure you've got something very interesting to say to all of us," he said with a snide smile.

God this bastard! I felt like wanting to scream, but I couldn't do that. I needed to keep things chill, let him continue this. And see how long I can last.

But then he pushed his fingers upward slightly, pressing up inside of me, and as he did that, I felt that surge of pleasure, that affection, everything just hit all at once. I let out a garbled sound, and then, as I did it, I cried out.

"What's the matter? Trying to hold back?" he said.

I was, but I could feel the whole thing slowly tearing me apart. He was getting a kick out of this, like it was a game for him. And I hated it.

"Care to give in?" he told me.

I gritted my teeth. There was no way in hell I was going to. I paused, looking into his eyes.

"I'm…not going to," I told him.

He then dipped his fingers in deeper. I was so close. I could feel the release just begging to come out as he moved himself, teasing, dipping his fingers deep into my pussy. I grasped the chains, holding them. I'm not going to let it get to me though.

But then he hit that area again, causing me to let out a small cry, holding my body, tensing up.

"You can back out at any time hun. Just say the word," he said.

Fuck. I was losing my goddamn mind. I gritted my teeth, trying to figure out what to do. Finally, I sighed.

"Alright, I'll...I'll do this," I told him.

He laughed, moving his hand away.

"Do what? I want to hear what you have to say," he said.

This rat bastard. I don't know why he has done this to me. I don't understand what his reason for this even is.

"I want you to...to take me," I told him.

"Alright, whatever you say," he said.

I looked at him, and then, he moved the chains away from the wall. He wasn't taking me out of them, was he? But then he flipped me over, so that my ass was hanging out in the air, and as I looked forward, I felt a hand on my ass.

"You have such a nice butt. I figured part of your punishment before I even gave you what you wanted would be this. Wouldn't it be fun?" he asked me.

His hands gripped me there, and I gasped.

"So, what are you going to do?" I asked him.

"Simple. I want to see you squirm of course, so I plan to spank you until you finally give me what I want. I want to hear the moans that you make, the delicious sounds that are uttered," he told me.

This man. He was trying so hard to get me to give in.

"Well you'll have to do more than that," I said.

"I guess if you give me enough incentive I will stop," he said.

This guy was enjoying this far more than I expected him to. He grabbed my ass, squeezing it once more, and then, he let out a low groan.

"Oh, this will be fun," he said.

I couldn't move, my hands and feet were in the chains, and there was something so annoying and yet...so damn thrilling about all of this that turned me on, that made me excited for him.

He then raised his hand, slowly slapping my ass with a hard hit.

When it made contact, I let out a garbled sound, shocked at how good this felt. He then smacked me again and again, hitting every single part of me, penetrating deep into the fibers of my being. There was a thrill there, a need for something more, and when he hit me with his hand, I knew that he was enjoying this far more than he cared to admit. He started to smack me once again, this time hitting me with all his might, causing me to let out a small gasp of surprise and pleasure, enjoying the touch this man bestowed upon me.

It was perfect, simply perfect, and I enjoyed the hell out of it.

He continued to hit me hard with his hands, each smack making me lose all semblance of control, enjoying the feeling of this, loving the touch of his hands.

But the sting was becoming more and more obvious.

He would make sure to hit right up against my pussy, causing me to let out a small moan of surprise, enjoying the touch of it. He then would hit it again, this time with much more force, causing me to let out a small, garbled sound.

"Fuck," I said.

"You want more slut?" he said.

"Do your worst," I said.

Then, I heard something bigger get grabbed. I paused, wondering just what this man would bring out. then, I felt it right up against my ass, causing me to let out a howl of both pain and pleasure.

It was a pole. He was using it to hit me hard, and the caning started to make me grit my teeth. And yet, I found pleasure in it. Every touch made me shiver and cry out. He would purposefully move it right up against my glistening pussy, as if to tease me completely. I felt completely lost in the pleasure this man gave to me, and it was then when, after a few more moments he pulled this away, looking me in the eyes.

"There you go," he said.

I whimpered, turned on and ready for whatever he would give to me next. He would continue this, but I was losing it. I felt sore, but mostly I just wanted him to…to just take me completely and make me feel good.

He hit me one last time, causing a howl to come out of me. Then, he rubbed the cane against my folds.

"What was that?" he said with a tease.

I gritted my teeth, feeling frustrated by the way that he was teasing me. I wanted him to just outright take me and fuck me mercilessly, but I couldn't just say that. The last thing I wanted was to give him the goddamn satisfaction.

But maybe that's what he wanted. Maybe he just…wanted to see how far he could take it. I wondered this, but then he pushed the cane deeper against me, his hand touching my pucker and also rubbing the red there.

"Well, what do you say? Ready to give in yet?" he asked me with a purr.

Did I want to give in? Well, the horny part of me wanted him to just take me and turn me into the quivering little slut that he wanted, but there was that other part of me that was just begging to hold on a little while longer.

I took a deep breath, steeling myself for the next part, when I spoke.

"Take me," I whimpered.

"What was that?"

Fuck he was trying to completely tease me, making me his little bitch, and then, I sighed.

"Please take me," I said.

"I can't hear you. You're a little quiet there," he said.

Ugh, this bastard! I then sighed, looking over at him and then speaking.

"Fuck me! Please! I fucking need it," I said.

He then gave me one loud smack, causing me to let out a small moan of pleasure, and then I saw him smile.

"You want it so badly huh?"

"Yes," I breathed out, barely able to get my shit together.

"Then go on ahead. Let's really make this fun now," he said to me.

I watched as he spread me apart, looking me in the eyes, and then, shortly thereafter, he soon pushed all the way in, hitting that spot deep within me.

I let out a small cry, holding onto him, watching as he slid his cock deep within, and then back out again. He then looked me in the eyes, smiling.

"You good?" he asked me.

"Amazing," I breathed out.

But the truth was, I felt like I was about to lose my mind, and I couldn't help but wonder if there was more to this as well. He then grabbed my legs, spreading me apart, pushing in deep and making me shiver and cry out.

I grabbed onto him, holding him as he rammed his cock into me, but he made sure not to hit that one spot. He was trying to get me to beg to cum.

He was driving a hard bargain.

"Please," I whimpered as he continued to thrust.

"Please what? I'm getting close you know," he said.

Of course he fucking was. I started gritting my teeth once again, planning to scream out the feelings that I had, and what I wanted.

"Please just let me cum already!" I cried out.

He looked at me, seeing how needy I was, and then, he laughed.

"Well since you asked so nicely…here we go then," he said.

He then pushed his hands upward toward my breasts, pinching and teasing my nipples as he angled his cock, hitting my g-spot. I held the chains, feeling the limited movement change the way things were.

I wanted nothing more than to be taken completely, to enjoy the touch and the feeling of this, and as he held me, thrusting himself deep within me, I could feel my whole body practically tense up, losing control, and then, I held him, cumming hard against him.

I felt the orgasm shatter every fiber of my being. I screamed out, loving everything about this, and it was then when, after a few more thrusts he then groaned and held me, filling me up completely.

I didn't expect his seed to be pumped all the way into me, but I was completely at the mercy of this man.

I loved every moment of this though. And as he finished, he pulled out of me, the cum dripping from my pussy. I was completely enthralled by the way that this felt, and for a second, I simply sat there, looking at him. He then gave me a small smile.

"There we go," he said to me.

"But…what now?" I asked him.

"What do you mean? You're free to go," he said.

He undid the chains, pulling them off of my body. I could feel my hands again, which was pretty nice. But as I looked at him, I had many more questions than answers.

"Why though?" I asked him.

"Why what?"

"Did you…let me go. After all this time," I told him.

He paused, and then, he shrugged.

"Maybe I just felt like being nice. I wanted to…make sure that you were taken care of," he told me.

I flushed, but then I nodded.

"Thank you," I said to him.

"Not a problem. I just want to see you do well, and I'm happy I can be there for you," he said to me.

I looked into his eyes, and then I nodded.

"Thank you," I said to him.

"You're most welcome. I'm sure this is something that you will definitely remember me for," he told me.

I smiled, happy and amazed at how good this was. I then looked around, wondering just what in the world would happen next. I was a bit shocked that he was doing all of this to be nice to me, and I was definitely thankful for this.

He finished getting the chains off of me, but then, he looked me in the eyes.

"Don't tell anyone about this. Got it?" he said.

"But   why   not?"
"Because I want this to be kept as our little secret. If the guards find out...I'll be in deep shit. So don't let anyone else know what happened here," he said.

The way his voice cut as he said those words made me realize just the significance of this. I then nodded.

"Alright, I'll do that," I told him.

"Good. I think that settles it. Now, don't tell anyone about this. I let you go because I pitied you. The truth is...I don't agree with the kingdom, and I don't like it, and I'm not that happy about it. But it's not like there is much I can do. So, I'm telling you right now, if you want things to go well, you should just let things go, and go from there," he said to me.

I paused, realizing he was doing this because he wanted to help me. Maybe he was on my side. There were many parts of the revolution who didn't have the guts to admit it.

And maybe he was one of those that did admit it deep down. I beamed, and then I spoke.

"Alright, keep this between us then," I said.

"Fair," he told me.

I got ready to leave, and then, as I got myself together, he was then gone. A part of me wishes that he stuck around. That he could...possibly work something out with me. Maybe he could assist me in the revolution, as a spy of sorts.

But I should be glad he didn't kill me, that he was letting me go. And as I looked around, I realized that getting out of this cell would be easier said than done.

"Shit, where to now?" I said.

It didn't help that I was naked too. He ripped all of my clothes. But to the right of me were some linens. I grabbed them, putting them on. Then, I saw some armor, left there in the corner.

Did he leave this on purpose? Or was it from someone else? Either way, I was thankful for the armor. I put it on my body, checking to see how I looked, smiling excitedly as I looked forward.

"There we go. We should be ready to go now," I told myself.

I was excited for this, ready to face the future. I saw that nobody was looking around, so I made my way up to the foyer, and then made a break for the entrance.

I didn't stick around to see what the guards would say about me, good or bad. But I was just relieved to know that I had my freedom once again. But a part of me wondered if there was a reason for this, or even what else I could do.

But I would miss him... even though I knew getting involved with a guy like that wasn't good for me, I wanted to. I wanted to find him again, and possibly...continue where we left off.

But I wasn't sure if it was possible. But I hoped that one day, he'd possibly continue to be the revolutionary that he wanted to be, and he'd come work with me, no matter what happened next.

Seeing Daddy

Daddy Domination, Roleplay

I sat there, waiting on the bed for him to call me. I knew for a fact that he was waiting for me, ready to see me put on a little show for him.

Daddy.

I felt a bit of excitement as I looked forward. Sometimes I didn't totally get into the little space aspects of this, but right now…I just wanted daddy to come in and have his way with me.

But alas, daddy, my boyfriend Quinn, was busy until 11. He told me to get into something nice and ready for him, so that's what I did. I wore a pink negligee, a little set of black stockings, and put my hair in cute pigtails. It let me be the "Princess" that I knew I could be. And it was a kink that I often loved to explore.

I wanted him to just take me and have his way with me, but I knew that may be too much to ask of him. However, maybe I could at least goad him a little bit.

I prepared the text message, and the video call, my body and mind excited to hear his voice. I sent it out, my fingers a little bit nervous as I pulled the trigger.

The truth is, I was always kind of a vanilla person until I met Quinn. Then, he showed me daddy domination. At first, I was a little bit nervous about doing this, but after he showed me a few things, there was a thrill, and excitement that came from this whole thing.

And I wanted to see just what would happen.

I simply sent it out.

Video call me daddy!

And then I waited. Moments later he sent over a text, asking why. And I smiled.

I had something to show him.

And that's what I said. Personally, I was a little bit nervous about doing this. It would be the first time we did this sort of thing while he was at work.

Quinn worked in a prominent law office as one of the main lawyers. Which meant he had to keep a very low profile with this sort of thing. But I felt the thrill. The excitement and the desire washed over me as this continued to happen.

I waited a little bit until of course, I heard his voice.

"What are you doing Patty?"

"I just had a surprise for you," I told him.

"Like what…."

"Turn on the video and you'll see it," I said with a smile.

There was hesitation, and then, moments later he did so, fumbling with the camera before turning it on. I watched as he sat there, in his perfectly pressed lawyer suit, looking at me with an annoyed face.

"Patty please, you know I'm trying to finish up."

"But daddy, I'm ready for you now," I said, biting my lip.

"Come on Patty, you know I can't—"

"Can't I at least show you how much I want you?" I asked him.

There was a long pause, and then, moments later, he sighed.

"Fine. You can do that," he said.

But the tone of his voice didn't fit the rest of it. I smiled, excited for what this may mean for us. I spread myself on the bed, looking at him as I bit my lip.

"Like...this," I said.

I rubbed my entrance, watching his face contort into an obvious poker face.

"Daddy, I want you to come home. You promised you would," I told him.

"I know but I need to finish and—"

I let out a small moan, touching myself as I moved my hand against my folds as I looked at him.

"Come on daddy, you should know by now that this is what you're looking for," I said to him. He looked at me, biting his lip slightly as he spoke.

"I can't do this yet Patty."

"But I can't hold back daddy. I want you nowwww," I told him.

I started to rub myself, moving my fingers, watching as his eyes widened and his mouth dropped. I started to rub my finger against my clit, letting out a small sigh of need as I touched myself. I was horny and needy, aching for him as I continued to feel my body tense up, the desire, need, and lust growing within.

"Come on daddy, can't you take a little bit of time off?" I said.

"You know I can't and—"

I started rubbing myself more, my hands against my nipple. I let out a small gasp, needing something inside me. I wanted him to just quit, to come home and take care of me. I began to slide my fingers in, biting my lip as I looked up.

"I'm thinking of you, daddy," I told him.

"Really now?" he said.

"Yes, I want you to come home, to pound me, and to make me quiver and shiver. I can only take care of myself for so long," I purred.

"I see," he said.

I began to rub myself a little bit harder, watching his body start to struggle. He was hard. That's the face he made when he was turned on, and I smiled, excited to see more.

"Come onnnn daddy," I told him.

He sighed, realizing he wasn't going to get anywhere with this. He then took a deep breath, looking into my eyes.

"Fine. You win," he replied.

I beamed, looking at him, excitedly.

"There you go. I can't wait for you," I said.

"I'll be back when it's time," he told me.

I knew that's what he did. There was something fun, thrilling, and exciting about all of this. I smiled a devilish grin, enjoying the way he looked at me awkwardly.

Without another word, he turned off the video call. I pouted.

"He could've at least waited for me to say bye. But oh well," I muttered to myself.

I sat there, frustrated at the lack of his presence. I just wanted daddy here now. I started to sit there, spreading my legs, touching myself as I thought about him.

"Daddy…."

I continued to stroke myself against my panties. I'm sure this would be one hell of a sight. I was excited to say the least, and I was definitely ready for whatever would happen next.

I then continued to move my hands, daintily touching myself, enjoying the touch, moaning his name, when suddenly, I heard the car pull up.

Damn Quinn got home fast. I guess he couldn't take it. That's what he gets for ignoring me when I needed him the most.

"Come on daddy…give me some fun," I told myself.

I started pulling my panties downward, grabbing my favorite toy. It was a vibrator, about the size of daddy's cock, and as I started to turn it on, feeling the vibrations within me, I sat there, holding myself against the bed.

"Oh, daddy, please. Please fill me up," I said.

I started moving the toy against my body, imagining it was him. His rough hands holding me, grabbing my arms, and dominating me as he fucked me senseless. Feeling his hands against my throat, and I started to feel my whole body tense up, feeling the excitement wash over me.

I continued to hold the toy, pushing it deeper within. Every part of this was making me lose my mind, filling me up even more, and I knew that from everything that was going on that it was only a matter of time.

Each and every single touch sent me shivering, making me ache for more and wanting him completely. I felt my hands move slightly, pressing the toy right up against my clit.

I was so damn close. I knew that I needed to last, but maybe if I just had a little orgasm...

"What are you doing?" he said.

I turned to him, flushing crimson as he looked at me, seeing the toy in my hands, and a wry smile on my face.

"Sorry, daddy. I've been a very naughty girl," I said out loud.

"I can see that. You were getting off without me. That's something that I told you that you shouldn't do, remember? We had that agreement. And I saw that you were very close to orgasm there," he said to me.

I flushed but then nodded.

"Sorry daddy," I told him.

It was a struggle. I couldn't just sit there and wait for him, right.

But then, instead of responding, he went over, grabbed the paddle, and looked at me.

"Remember what we agreed upon. If you're a bad girl for daddy, you will get punished," he said.

Damn. He was already trying to make me feel more frustrated. I knew that this punishment was coming, but then, I smiled, curling my lips into a Cheshire cat grin.

"Make me."

Those were the two words that would make him respond. He quickly pushed me down on the bed, thrusting me on all fours. I shivered, enjoying the touch, and the way that he simply took over. He then grabbed my ass, massaging the cheeks.

"What was that? I thought we talked about that little mouth of yours princess?" he said.

"I said make me! I wanted to get off, what are you going to do about it and—"

Then he smacked me with the paddle, making me cry out. it felt good because I could get off to spankings, but also, I didn't really enjoy it.

"Well, princess? I'm waiting," he said.

He then smacked me again and again, causing me to let out a small gasp, enjoying the sensation and pleasure. Every single touch, every single motion, they were all driving me to the point of need, of desire, and making me want even more. He then hit me harder once more.

"Ahh, daddy!" I cried out.

"You get three more spankings for being such a naughty girl," he said.

I wiggled my butt, excited for it. He grabbed the paddle, hitting that one part of my body that made me shiver and cry out, sending me soaring, making me ache for him, and wanting him, to just take me and use me like the naughty girl that I was.

He continued to do this, every little touch sending me to the edge, making me want more, crave more, excited for the rest of it. After the third spanking, my ass felt raw, and then, he put me on my back, looking at me.

"So princess, what did you need that was so important you had to interrupt me from work?" he said.

"I just wanted your cock daddy," I told him, smiling as I spread my legs, my pussy wet with desire.

He cupped my chin and looked me in the eyes. His eyes said he was bothered and lusting for me, but the way his face looked, he pretended to be annoyed with me.

"Daddy said you shouldn't disobey the rules. You couldn't stop thinking about me though, could you?" he said.

"No daddy, I wanted to feel your cock inside of me," I told him.

He let out a small chuckle, moving his hand away from my chin, taking a moment to drink up the sight of me. I knew that this was what daddy wanted.

He seemed to be curious about this too. His hands moved towards my breasts, touching and teasing them, looking me in the eyes.

"Look at you, so turned on like the little slut that you are. I can't believe you, princess," he said.

"Daddy, I can't get enough of you. I want you," I told him. And I meant that as well. This wasn't me just bullshitting either, and it was obvious that he enjoyed this too.

"Well, daddy is going to give you a hard dicking, and he's getting out the restraints too since you of course decided to disobey him," he said with an admonished tone.

There was something so fucking hot about being told no like this. Maybe it was the fact that he was saying it to me like this, but I was so fucking hot and bothered that I couldn't get enough of it, and I ached for it.

"Well maybe I want that then daddy," I said.

He grabbed my hands, holding them above my head hard, but not so hard that it hurt me. He looked me in my eyes and then smiled before crushing his lips to my own.

The domineering, amazing kiss was enough to drive me crazy, and I thrust my hips upward.

He then grabbed something with his free hand, putting one of them through the bars of the headboard, and the other one binding my tiny hands together.

"There we go, you won't be going anywhere for now," he said to me.

"But I don't want to go anywhere, daddy. I want you," I said.

He looked me in the eyes, laughing.

"I can see. You've become such a needy slut for me that I can see it in your eyes. So tell me, what do you want daddy to do to you? Do you want him to tease you like this," he said to me.

His hands moved downward, touching my sides, making me cry out slightly. His hands moved down, touching the wet part of my panties, looking up at me.

"So wet already. You really are a slut, over here thinking about daddy like this," he said.

"Ahh yes," I told him.

I meant those words too. There was something so damn thrilling about this. I don't know why, but I wanted him to take me, to use me like the little princess that I was, and to be taken advantage of like this.

He then moved down to my feet. Fuck not there. He moved his hands downward, touching the bottom of my feet, my toes curling in response.

"Look at you. Already so damn turned on, completely at the mercy of my hands and my touches," he said to me.

I whimpered, completely turned on by the little touch. See...daddy knew that I liked the sensitive parts of my body touched. It didn't even need to be my pussy or tits, it could just be my feet, or even my armpits and sides, and I would become a panting, whimpering mess in front of him. And this of course was no exception.

He continued to smile, touching and teasing every single part of me, enjoying the way that this felt, and I couldn't help but enjoy it. I started to feel him press his hands to the bottom of my feet, touching and teasing me there, and I started to enjoy the feeling even more.

But as soon as I started to feel pleasure, he stopped, moving his hands upward, touching the inner parts of my thighs, letting his hands graze against the tip of my pussy, moving along the sides. That's when I let out a cry, and he of course, laughed at the sounds that I made.

"Just look at you. Such a mess already. Turned on and a little slut as well. My, you must be enjoying this," he told me.

"I...I am," I told him, completely in a rapturous moment, enjoying everything that came from him.

His hands then skirted upward, moving toward the tip of my breasts, touching them slightly. He looked me in the eyes, seeing the lustful look, and then he spoke.

"I didn't expect you to wear something so cute. Were you waiting to wear this for daddy? To take it off of you?" he said.

"Yes daddy," I told him.

I picked this out for him since I knew it was his favorite color, and he smiled.

"What a good princess. Always so sweet and supportive of me too. I love that," he said.

He reached upward, letting his fingers touch against the very tips of my nipples, rubbing his hands there, watching me moving the tip, letting his fingers rub slightly. But I knew that I was losing my mind.

I started to feel his hands move under my top, moving against my nipples, pinching and teasing them. He also let one of his fingers rest against my armpits, touching there slightly.

That's when I let out a sigh, completely and utterly lost in the feeling of this, enjoying his touch. I knew that he was enjoying this as much as I was, and that every single touch was enough to drive me crazy.

He continued these touches, listening to the sounds that came out of me.

"So what's going on princess? Enjoying this?" he asked me.

"Yes," I said out loud.

"Yes, what?"

"Yes, daddy. I love this," I told him.

It was what I had waited for. There was something about the way that Quinn touched me that made me become putty in his hands.

Usually, I wouldn't let him have all the fun, and I would try to take a little bit of control as well, but then, he continued to press his fingers there, causing me to let out a small series of gasps and sighs, enjoying the touch.

He did this for a bit, watching me slowly come undone, when he pulled away, looking me in the eyes, seeing the need, the whole feeling, and the pleasure that came out of this.

"Well? What do you think? Are you going to be a good girl?" he said to me.

"Yes," I told him.

"Yes, what? I won't continue until I hear it from your lips," he teased.

That motherfucker.

"Yes, daddy. I will be a good girl.

He soon smiled, pressing right up against the very tip of my pussy. He rubbed there, making me enjoy every single moment of this. It was so enjoyable, that I couldn't help but love everything that came from this as well. I soon moved my body towards his touches, realizing that he was still teasing me, forcing me orgasm denial as well.

"Please, give me more," I told him.

"You're going to have to beg a little bit harder than that," he said to me.

Fuck, I couldn't help but ache for him, and I needed him. I started to push my legs forward, moving my body so that it was right there, waiting for him. I soon started to feel his hands move towards the inner part of my panties, going underneath, and then moments later stroking my folds. Every touch was making me whimper, and when he pushed two fingers inside, I let out a small gasp of surprise, enjoying everything that came from this. For a moment, I simply just laid there, basking in everything, enjoying the touches.

He then stopped, right as I was about to cum, causing me to let out a small groan of annoyance. I wanted him to just take me right then and there. He smiled.

"Well, do you want more? Because I can leave you like this," he teased.

"No daddy, I want this. Please…I need it," I told him, moaning out loud at the notion of this. I didn't expect this to just completely destroy me in the ways that it was. And yet, I loved it. I loved being taken like this by him, completely at the mercy of his touches, and then, after a brief second, he laughed.

"Alright. Good girl then," he said.

He soon pushed his hands towards my panties, rubbing down there, pushing in and out first with one finger, and then with multiple fingers, making me suddenly lurch and moan in response to this. I was already losing control, enjoying everything that came out of this, and it was then when, moments later, he pulled my panties down and off.

I was so close already that I groaned in mild annoyance at the feeling of this. But then, moments later, he moved towards me, looking me in the eyes as he smiled.

"Well, do you plan on begging for it?"

"Yes daddy, give me your cock, please," I said.

He laughed, and then undid his pants. I expected him to thrust it into me, making me feel the effects of it all, but then moments later, he moved his cock towards my mouth, pushing it in and watching his eyes start to widen. He choked me with his cock, and I felt the large member hit the back of my mouth, causing me to let out a garbled sound of pure pleasure, the enjoyment of such making me feel turned on and happy about it.

He continued to gag me on his cock, and I enjoyed everything that came from this. Every single touch, it was all just...so damn perfect, and he didn't seem to want to stop it.

He got his cock to the back of my mouth, holding it there as I gagged on it. He then pulled back out, making me catch my breath. He grabbed my chin, pulling it upwards.

"Does my little princess want my cock," he asked me.

"Yes, daddy. I would love that," I told him.

And I meant it. He then smiled, pulling my face back, and it was only moments later when I felt him spread me apart, causing my breath to hitch.

Would he be hard and make me lose it? Or would he be gentle? Something told me that he had planned to be hard and ruthless with me. And yet, I loved everything about that. He slowly pressed himself deep into me, making me suddenly gasp with surprise, amazed at how good this was. He soon pressed in and out, enjoying everything that came out of my mouth. And I of course, enjoyed the feeling too.

Every touch, every caress, every single press inside was enough to drive me to the brink. He held me there, but then, as soon as he was about to hit that spot, the one location that would make me orgasm, he stopped.

"What's the matter, princess? You want something?"

Fuck, I knew what he wanted. Me to beg of course. I flushed crimson, and then moments later I said it.

"Choke me…daddy. I want to feel your cock," I said to him.

I loved it when he choked me out. He wrapped his fingers around the spot on my neck, causing my eyes to widen and the pleasure to surge through me.

"Then my little princess will have that," he said.

He then thrust inside, causing me to let out little gasps and sounds of pleasure. He hit right up against my G-spot, causing me to howl in pleasure as I felt the throes of my orgasm hit me. I thought that he would join me, but he didn't.

No, after I came, he stopped for a moment, touching my hair for a second, and then smiling.

"Don't worry, I'll take good care of you," he said to me.

He then started to move his cock in and out of me, pressing right up against that spot, and it was only then when I cried out, feeling my whole body start to lose control, and it was only then when I felt him hit right up against there.

Moments later, I felt my whole body just tense up. He pressed his lips to my own, holding me there, and it was then when I let out a small, garbled sound, cumming hard against him as he filled me up with his cum.

He then finished up, pulling away, and looking at me. I was spent, my vision blurred, my whole body completely wasted and amazed at how I was able to stay conscious throughout all of this. He then touched my head, smiling.

"You good there, princess?" he asked me.

I nodded.

"Yeah…I think I am," I told him.

In truth, I didn't know how to register any of this. But then he reached for the restraints, undoing them and putting them off to the side. I looked into his eyes, and for a long time, we didn't say a word. Then, he grabbed my favorite stuffed animal, giving that to me.

"Here you go. Cuddle that while I get you some water," he said.

"Thanks, daddy," I told him.

Quinn beamed, and then left for a moment. Moments later, he came back with some cookies, and of course some water for me. I drank it, eating a couple of the cookies that he brought me. He simply touched my hair, looking me in the eyes as he spoke.

"How are you feeling?" he asked.

How was I feeling? I felt like I'd been hit by a train, but also, I really enjoyed everything that he gave to me. Even though he was rough, there was something thrilling about the rough nature of this, and then, I spoke.

"I'm pretty good. That was just pretty amazing," I told him.

"You liked it?"

"Of course, daddy. I loved every second of it," I told him.

He breathed out a sigh of relief as he heard me say that.

"Okay good. I wanted to make sure that I wasn't too rough on you or anything. Just when I saw you there, teasing me like that, it was turning me on and I felt like I needed to be there right then and there," he told me.

"Yeah true," I told him.

"Anyways, I think we're good. Do you want me to go and make you some food?"

"Sure daddy. Or I can try to move in a bit and—"

"Don't worry about it. I've got it," he insisted.

I looked into his eyes, seeing the serious expression there. Damn, he really meant it.

"Okay, daddy. Thanks," I said.

"Not a problem. Everything is in place for my little princess to have a good time," he said.

I smiled, leaning in and giving him a long, passionate kiss. I really did like him, and he was a big part of my life. I just had no clue what else to do at this point, other than to stay with him and to be with him.

For a long time, I simply relished in it. But then he went down to make me some food. And I sat there, thinking about what I did, and the fun that I had just had.

I would do it again. I would totally tease him again, and I knew from the way that he was talking that he enjoyed this as much as I did. I thought about it, and about what he felt.

In a strange way, I personally felt good about all of this. I looked over at my phone, seeing the video call that I had with Quinn. Even though he was frustrated, it seemed like he channeled that frustration of course, into something a whole lot more fun. And when I touched to view the video, I smiled to myself.

"I can't wait to have fun like this again," I said.

I moved downwards, touching myself, rubbing off quickly to the idea of Quinn teasing me like that again. He was a good dom. Someone who knew when to stay in his lane, and he never overstepped the boundaries that he had. There was something good about that, which made me realize that I could trust him.

I quickly finished myself off, taking my hands and rubbing quickly. Moments, later, I let out a small groan, finishing up. When he came back, he saw me there, and he simply smiled.

"You good there princess?" he asked me.

"Amazing daddy. I was just sitting here, waiting for you to come," I said.

He leaned in, giving me a strong kiss, and one that was quick too.

"Well, I sure as shit hope you didn't have to wait long. I made your favorite food. I figured you'd need this after the adventures that we shared together," he told me with a smile.

I quickly saw the food, taking it and beaming towards him as I dug in. It tasted amazing, just the way that daddy liked to do it, and I enjoyed every passing moment of it. He laughed as he saw me wolf it all down, touching my shoulders slightly, looking me in the eyes.

"I can only hope to give you something that you will enjoy, and something that you will remember from here on out," he said.

He was my daddy, someone that I could trust, and someone who took care of me. I knew that this was a different type of dynamic, but I could tell from the way that Quinn interacted with me that he enjoyed this. He then rubbed my back as he ate, whispering little sweet nothings into my ear. I quickly let out a small moan, pushing myself down next to him, and he simply smiled.

"I just want to give you what's best for you, what my little girl deserves, and something to remember me by," he said.

I smiled, thankful for that.

"Oh, don't worry daddy, I don't think I could ever forget you, you know," I told him.

He laughed, giving me another kiss, and I leaned in against him, feeling safe and secure near him. I knew that I could trust Quinn, no matter what the odds may be. He was someone that I adored, someone that I could rely on no matter what, and someone I was falling for every single day.

The Business Trip

MILFs, Gangbang

It was time.

One of the first business trips I would have with my department. We were going to Vegas, and the company was paying for the whole trip, plus I got a small little allowance every single day.

Not only that, but I also definitely needed a break. They told me I'd be going with my group, so I'd have to work with the people in my department.

The thing is, I haven't seen them at all.

I wondered what it was that they were up to. We did most of the work online, so most of the time it didn't really apply to us to all meet up. This would be the first time we'd all meet for something like this.

And yet, there was something exciting about that.

I looked around, seeing where the group was. When I got there, I stopped, my eyes wide.

There was a group of attractive men in business suits that were all sitting there. They looked over at me, waving slightly.

"You're Beatrice, right?" one of them said.

"Yeah. And I'm assuming you guys are a part of the division?" I asked them.

They nodded.

"Yeah, I'm Henry, that's Caleb, that's Cody, and Dan is here too. We're just waiting on one more person. Maria," Henry explained.

I listened, but I was kind of lost in Henry's eyes. He was attractive as all hell, and he looked at me with a small smile, excitement in his eyes.

Fuck was I already lost in the feeling of this? Was this…. right though?

I couldn't help but already notice my head was in the clouds.

"You okay there?" the guy who I noticed as Caleb said. He had really attractive green eyes, a smile on his face, and when he looked at me, I couldn't help but feel the rush of excitement.

"Yeah, I'm okay," I told him.

"Alright. Well, if there's anything you want, please let me know," he said.

Besides his cock. But also, I didn't want it to be that type of trip. We all met, and each of the guys had something utterly unique about them, and yet…. I couldn't help but feel like I was enthralled, completely lost in the way that they spoke, enjoying the feeling of this too.

That's why I didn't want to let them know anything. Could I stop this? I didn't think so.

Then, the guys looked over at me, eying me up and down, causing me to flush crimson. There was something thrilling, exciting about this. Sure, it was probably going to be your average business trip, but a girl could dream, right?

That's when I saw her. Maria. She walked down towards all of us, and I flushed, realizing how pretty she was.

It was rare for women to get me to feel this way, and when I saw Maria there, she looked at me, giving me a wry little smile.

"Hey there everyone," she said.

"Hey yourself," I heard Henry say.

She gave them a wink, and then her eyes immediately focused on me. the way she stared into my eyes made my heart skip a beat and made me ache for her.

That's when it made me realize—holy shit this could become something real.

I started to flush, thinking about what could happen. But then she looked at me, giving me a small wink.

"I didn't know we'd have some female company on this trip. That's exciting," Maria said.

I knew Maria was one of the superior advisors in the company, but I didn't expect her here. I looked over at the guys, who were salivating over her, not that I blamed them though. She was gorgeous, and I felt both jealous, yet also kind of aroused.

"Yeah, nice to finally meet you," I told her.

"Same to you too. I've heard about you from the team. One of our star moms on the team," she said.

That's right. I did have a daughter named Clarisse. She's eight, and she's with her grandparents while I'm gone. Sadly, that's the last real big action I've gotten besides some disastrous hookups.

"Thank you," I told her.

"Course. I get it because I've got three kids myself. All a little older though," she told me.

So she was a mom too? That kind of made sense. The guys couldn't stop staring at both of us.

But it was best if we got started with settling in. I followed her out of there, making our way over to the hotel.

The first night was a simple dinner, but the bedroom eyes she kept giving me, and the way the guys looked at both of us was definitely exciting. I mean, it was something that was on the forefront of my mind, but I also kind of wondered what they thought about all of this too.

For a long time, we all just sat around, all of us talking and enjoying one another, the excitement in our bones. I could sense that there was tension though.

The next day was business meetings. Again, the tension was so thick you could cut through it with a knife. And yet, there was something about the way that she continued to look at me which made me shiver, and I wanted to just ask her what she had planned.

But I feared what may come about from that.

Oh well, no sense in getting worked up over it.

That evening though, I got a text from Maria, saying that she got us all a place to party. I asked her what she meant, and she said that we should celebrate, simply because it's been one hell of a journey.

I decided to tag along. After all, it's not like I didn't like the idea of it. I wore a simple black dress, walked into the building and headed to where Maria had this all set up.

When I got there, she was dressed in a suit that hugged her curves, just barely hiding anything. I flushed looking over at her, realizing that she did something to me.

"What's up?" she asked.

"Well...I was thinking we could have a little bit of fun here. You know, something to truly remember what we're doing here," she said.

"What do you...mean by that?" I said.

I looked around the place. It was a meager room, a space with of course, a bed for the most part. The sheets were red, and I noticed a long couch somewhere around here. Why did I get a feeling that this was something that she had planned for a while? Maybe I was overthinking this, but she looked at me, smiling.

"Tell you what, why don't you have a seat, Henry, David, Caleb, and Dan will be here in a minute," she said.

I nodded, listening to Maria's words. I sat down, but I couldn't shake the fact that her eyes were looking at my body as if assessing something. I flushed thinking about it.

Stay calm. You don't want to get too excited.

As they all came in, they sat at each of the different seats, and of course, Marie was at the helm. The strong, confident demeanor that she had was such a turn-on, and when she looked at me, she gave me a small smile.

"So how are you feeling?"

"Good. But what is this?" I asked her.

"Simple. We were thinking of celebrating. We're all away from the office, and there isn't anyone to stop us or to bother us," she said.

"What do you mean by that?" I asked her.

She leaned forward, grabbing my chin, holding it there, and looking me in the eyes.

"I know you've been staring at me for quite a while sweetie. It's quite obvious. And Henry and the others told me the same too. That you would steal looks. And I don't blame you, perhaps you have a little crush on them? But isn't it hard for you to truly experience stuff like this, since you're taking care of a kid the whole time," she said.

Fuck, was she trying to tease me? I felt a bit embarrassed by this, but then nodded.

"Yeah, I mean...you are attractive and all and—"

I noticed all of the guys staring at me, and I noticed as well that Caleb was moving his legs back and forth, putting his hands through his blonde hair. Dan kept a very placid look on his face, as if analyzing something. David and Henry both had chill smiles, looking at me with a curious glance, as if wondering just what in the world we'd plan next.

"So, what do you say? Wouldn't it be...kind of fun to experience something different? With one another? Perhaps this could be something that you enjoy," she said.

"You mean like...all of us together?" I asked.

"Bingo. But that depends. Are you ready for it?" she asked.

I flushed. I had a feeling she would try to solicit something like this out of me. I began to feel my face redden, and I knew that she was enjoying this as much as I was.

"Well, that depends. If you want this too. I wouldn't mind it," I said.

Deep down, I did crave the idea of being treated like a little slut.

"Well tell you what, why don't the guys show you around a little bit. I want to watch, to see how far you go. And don't worry, this is between all of us, so if you end up enjoying this, it will be kept a secret," she said.

I sighed in relief, enjoying the fact that she wanted to keep this a secret. That was relieving to say the least. But then, I felt Henry step forward, taking my hand and giving me a wink with his soft blue eyes.

"Get on the bed," he insisted.

I flushed, but then did so, laying down on the bed. Henry, David, Caleb, and Dan all got up, following me to the bed. Before I knew it, Henry's hands were on my sides, moving towards my head, cupping my chin, and looking me in the eyes.

Fuck he was attractive, but my thoughts were soon silenced by the kiss that he gave me. it was soft and sweet, but also something succulent and fun, and I certainly was a bit surprised by this. I kissed him passionately, lost in the touch. Then moments later, Dan grabbed my chin, pulling me over to him. He still had the placid face that he had before, but his lips were strong, domineering, and I could barely keep up. I let out a small cry, enjoying the touch of this, craving more from this guy.

Then, there was David, who gave me a small little smile. He gave me a kiss, which was wetter than I thought, and I quickly enjoyed it, kissing him back, loving everything about this, wanting more from him as he did this. He stayed like this, his tongue greedily touching and teasing mine.

Then of course, there was Caleb, who after I felt David pull away, grabbed my chin and then kissed me. He was the youngest, so he felt the most inexperienced. But the kiss still was nice, and it helped me explore him. As we stayed like this, his tongue came forward, enjoying my own, and I quickly realized that I liked this as much as he did.

We all enjoyed the kiss for a bit, and I could see Maria sitting there, crossing her legs and giving me a smile that said it all.

"Come on, I know all of you guys wanted her. Give her something to remember you all by," she said.

Then, that's when I felt it. A hand move toward my shirt, undoing the buttons, pulling it off my body. I gasped, feeling my whole body slowly get exposed. I shivered, enjoying the touch of this as I noticed their bodies move closer.

That's when I noticed Henry's hands move downward, along with his lips. I noticed David and Dan's hands touch me too, exploring my body with the littlest of touches. Caleb also was curious, but he moved back, studying the scene in front of me. Henry moved towards my bra, touching my nipples with his hands, looking me in the eyes as he spoke.

"You do have the nicest tits you know. I have thought about it before," Henry said.

The confession alone was a turn-on. I'd be lying if I said I didn't want this, especially with the way his hands seemed to skillfully touch me, moving his hands around my body, and then, moments later, he pushed his hands to the back of my bra, touching my back. He looked at me for a moment to see if I wanted that, and then, he undid the clasp, holding it as he looked into my eyes, seeing if I wanted it.

And I sure as fuck did. He pulled off the cups, tossing it to the side with the rest of my clothes, his hands reaching forward to touch my breasts, moving his hands there. As she did so, I let out the smallest of moans, feeling completely lost in the touch of this man.

"What's the matter? You enjoying this?" he said, letting his fingers dance and graze around.

I was. I was very much enjoying this, and I knew that he was smiling as he did this, the subtle touch enough to make me lose my mind. His hands continued to dance for a bit, until both Dan and David moved him away.

"No fair quit hogging her to yourself," David said.

"Yes, this isn't just you Henry," I heard Dan say coldly.

"Sheesh, sorry guys. Fine, you can have a turn," he said.

I looked at them, and David moved his hands against one of my nipples and pinched it slowly. I gasped and held the edge of the bed, completely lost in the pleasure of this experience, and as he did this, he looked me in the eyes.

"You're so docile already. How cute," he said.

Then there was Dan, who seemed disinterested at the onset, but as he continued this, he gave me that glowering look, the one that screamed he wanted this too. There was clearly something more there, a desire, that was both raw and passionate, and as he continued to move his hands there, he pinched my nipple hard, making me shiver and moan with delight, enjoying this too.

I watched them both smile, and there was clearly a need for more, a desire to experience all of this, and then, moments later, I felt the hand pull on my nipple hard, pinching it, making me suddenly feel the pleasure from this. David pressed his lips to my nipple, touching it, and I rolled my eyes to the back of my head, completely in awe.

As he did this, I felt a pair of hands against my thighs, touching me, and when I managed to finally look down, I saw Caleb there, giving me a cheeky look.

"Want more princess?" he said.

"Yes," I panted, feeling my body relax. His hands moved towards me, moving up my legs, tugging at my skirt, and looking forward.

"Then allow me to show you something that you will enjoy then," he purred.

I looked at him, unsure of what he meant by that, but then, moments later, he pulled my skirt off, and then moved his hands to my panties, pulling them off too. I looked at him, and shortly after, he lifted my legs up, letting his tongue dart inside of me.

I grabbed the sheets, but moments later, before I could make a sound, I felt Henry right over me. Caleb's tongue was so skillful, touching and teasing me slowly, that I felt like I was at a loss on how to feel. Henry looked at me, licking his lips as he spoke.

"You look so delicious right now," he said.

"Ahh," I said.

He undid his pants, pulling out his cock, looking me in the eyes as he stroked it. He was sizable, and as I saw the underside of it throb for me, I licked my lips.

This was indeed what the fuck I wanted.

I opened my mouth, pressing my lips to his cock, sucking on it passionately, enjoying the touch of his cock against my lips. I began with kissing it at first, and moments later, I started sucking on the tip of it. The sounds that he made were delightful, and I felt like I could listen to those sounds again and again for as long as I could remember.

As he did this, I noticed Caleb's tongue move forward against my clit, holding onto it with his lips for a second, sucking on it. As he did that, I let out a small gasp, suddenly feeling completely mesmerized by the feeling of this. Moments later I felt my orgasm hit me, causing me to cry out, amazed by how good this was, and then, Henry pulled his cock out of my mouth with a pop. He touched my hair, looking at me.

As he did that, I noticed Dan and David both pulled away too, chucking off their pants, their cocks hard and throbbing. Dan was fucking huge, and I flushed thinking about that inside of me.

"Well, you ready for this? I want to feel inside of you," Henry said.

"You...do?" I said.

"Of course. You seem delightful, and I'm going to be the first one to pound you," he said.

I blushed as I heard those words, but then, Henry pulled away, and Caleb replaced him. He looked at me, nervous as all hell.

"I'm sorry this is the first time that I've done something like this," he said.

"It's alright. I'm just...nervous too. That's all," I told him.

He pulled his cock out slowly, and while it was smaller than Henry's, it still was quite girthy. I flushed thinking about how it would feel to have that inside my mouth.

As I felt his cock slowly enter me, I felt two of the cocks in my hand start to move, and I grabbed them, jerking them as I sucked on the cock there.

Then, I looked down and there was Henry. He had my legs spread, his cock right up inside of me. He touched me there, smiling.

"Not bad for someone who popped out a kid," he said.

I mean, it was years ago, but the thought was nice. I flushed.

"Thanks," I mumbled.

He smiled and chuckled, but not before pushing into me, filling me up with his cock. He slowly began to move, looking at me with a smile on his face as he began to move. I flushed, lightly gasping and groaning against the cock that was in my mouth.

This was so good, every touch of him sending shivers down my spine, making me lose every semblance of control as I did this. He continued to pound deep into me, and I was lost in the touch. Everything was so good.

He grabbed my hips, hiking my legs behind me, fucking me hard and raw, and after a few more thrusts, he looked up at me, groaning.

That's when I heard it, the sound of his last thrust, and then, the feeling of his seed spilling into me. I let out a gasp.

But as I did that, Caleb grabbed my face, holding me there, and shortly afterward, he thrust hard. I sat there, gobbling down his entire cock, completely lost in the touch, and then, when he got it deep into my mouth, let out a sigh of relief, filling deep within me.

His seed touched the back of my throat, making me gasp out in surprise and pleasure. For a long time, I simply just took it in, enjoying it, and then, moments later, he pushed his cock out of me, smiling as he looked me in the eyes.

"You good?" he asked.

I nodded, shocked at how...good it tasted, and how I felt.

But it wasn't over yet. Both David and Dan pulled away, and David looked at him.

"You thinking front or back?" Dan asked.

What were they talking about? Front and back? But then, I saw David smile.

"You can have front. I don't think she'd be able to take you from behind," he said.

What were they—

As soon as I was about to ask, I felt Dan pull me up, and shortly after, he plunged himself into me, making me scream out in pleasure as he moved himself in and out of me slowly.

But as he did that, I felt something behind me, and when it hit, I started to gasp.

It was a finger, but it didn't necessarily hurt. I figured that it was covered in lube, and as he plunged on in, I gripped the sheets, enjoying the rocking of fingers back and forth, moaning slightly as I felt the fingers plunge in a bit and as he hit there, I started to scream out, holding onto him, feeling good about everything as it continued to eat me fully.

The two fingers, followed by the third, moved against me, and then, as he plunged in further and further, I tensed up, moaning out loud. Dan continued to move in and out of me too, and I loved everything about this.

I let out a shiver, turning to David and looking him in the eyes.

"Give it…to me," I told him.

He looked me in the eyes, and then nodded.

"You sure?"

"Yes," I breathed out.

He nodded, pushing himself deep into me, and then, as he did so slowly, I shivered, moaning out loud, crying out softly, feeling good about everything. I started to let out a moan as he did this, pushing in his cock fully.

As I did that, I felt Dan plunge deep into me too. As I felt them both take me like this, I started to tense up, feeling like I was about to go insane with every single motion. I wanted them, and I wanted them to continue this.

After a few more thrusts, David grabbed my butt, thrusting it forward. As he did that, Dan started to move against me, thrusting upward too, hitting me in each spot. They continued this, and I was lost in the pleasure of this, enjoying it all. For a long time, I was loving everything about this, and then, after a few more moments, I noticed Maria get up, move toward me, and then, start to smile.

"There we go. Look at you, being used by all of your coworkers. You like this don't you?" she said.

"Yes," I cried out, feeling the throes of the pleasure that came from this.

"Well, maybe you could help me out too. Since I gave you this good little privilege," she said.

She slowly moved herself towards me, her pussy pushed in my face. I eagerly took it, and then, she pushed her face forward. I was buried in a bunch of muff, and then, she smiled. I used my tongue to tease her, and she pet my head.

"That's a good girl. You like this don't you?" she said.

I let out a small moan of surprise, and she soon pushed my face deeper. I pushed my tongue out, moaning against her crotch, and she smiled, rubbing her face there.

"That's a good girl. A very good girl," she said.

I let out a moan as a hand moved between my legs, touching me there, and then, moments later, I started to feel my whole body tense up. Dan then plunged into me, letting out a groan, spilling himself deep inside me, filling me up completely.

I loved this, being used by anyone and everyone. As he finished up, Dan looked me in the eyes, smiling.

"Damn you felt great," he said.

As he said that, he moved away, and then David started to move up and down, and then, moments later, I felt him let out a small groan. He let out a gasp as he filled me up completely.

Finally, there was Maria. Maria shoved my face into her pussy, rubbing against my mouth, and then, she let out a small moan, and seconds later, she let out a small gasp, cumming hard, holding me there. For a long time, she held my face there, smearing it completely with her juices.

I took a moment to experience all of this, completely amazed and feeling good about everything that she did. She moved away, looking me in the eyes.

I was spent. I felt like taking a nap or maybe ten as I started to look at them, moving away as I started to sigh. I felt good, completely spent, and she looked over at me, holding me there as she smiled. She then gave me a long, passionate kiss, and for a second, we stayed like this. I did love this, and when she pulled away, she grinned.

"That was fun," she said.

"Yeah, sure was," I finally breathed out.

"Good. I'm glad I could help you then," she said to me.

She gave me another kiss, and I smiled, excited to be there with her, and for a long moment, we stayed like this. She then moved back, smiling towards me.

"We could arrange this again you know," she said.

"But how?"

"I was thinking maybe…we could have another work meeting, and maybe we could bring them along. That would be good, right?" she said.

I turned to the guys, all of them sitting there and looking at me. I smiled, feeling good about everything.

"Sure, I'd like that," I said to them. They all smiled.

"Yes, but we should probably be heading back you know. We're supposed to be at a meeting in the morning" Henry said.

"True," Dan said.

"Well, maybe we can meet up once more before the end of the trip. I thought about this, and I knew that this was something that would be fun for all of us.

I wondered just what may happen next. Or if things would be good. But as they left, I saw Maria there, looking at me with a small smile.

"Well, how did you like that? I arranged it at the last minute, and I figured it would be good for you," she said to me.

"I really enjoyed it. Honestly. It was so different though from what I thought. I never expected all of them to well...want this sort of thing," I told her.

"What happens in Vegas dear," Maria told me.

She was right. This was something that we wouldn't talk about with anyone else, but it would be something that I would remember forever. I looked at her, and I then nodded.

"That is true. But what now?"

"Well, I would suggest that you definitely figure out what you want to do next. Maybe we can have a meetup at the end of next month or something. And you know, I always found you pretty cute," she said.

I flushed, thinking about that.

"You were the first…girl I've ever done that with," I told her.

"Well, you were quite fun to deal with as well," she said.

I flushed, and then nodded.

"Yes, it was. But I guess we should be going. I don't know…how long you have this place for," I told her.

"I'm not sure myself. But I can keep it around for a little bit, what do you think?" she said.

I nodded.

"That's true. I wouldn't mind…possibly exploring more of you too," I said.

She let out a low giggle, moving towards me and then cupping my chin and looking me dead in the eyes.

"Well, I'm sure we can continue to arrange that," she told me.

She pulled me toward the bed, giving me another long, passionate kiss. She tasted like strawberries, and I let out a small gasp of surprise and pleasure, enjoying myself. Everything felt fucking good, and that night, we made love on the bed, enjoying one another.

The next day, it was back to business. We went to the meetings we were supposed to, and I looked around at the rest of them, and they gave me a small smile.

I felt ready for this, and ready to do this again with them. But we had to keep it a secret. I was definitely excited to see where things would go, and how they would pan out.

We spent the rest of the trip like it was normal. Like we all didn't just have a whole massive gangbang in a random room that Maria put together.

But at the end of the trip, I noticed Maria give me a small wink as she boarded the plane.

My supervisor, someone who I never thought to be the type to do this sort of thing, did it, and I loved it. And as she left, she gave me a small note.

It just had some dates and a location on it, which probably indicated where the next one of these would be. Would she get involved in the next one? Or would it just be me?

Regardless, I felt excited about it. Sure, I did need to go back to my normal life, and Clarisse of course, but this was a trip that I would always remember, and it was obvious that what happens in Vegas will stay in Vegas, but it also will give me memories to remember it by, and I'll always remember the fun that I had here, and also the new experiences that I had with them, especially with the ones from my department.

And I would definitely do this again if given the chance.

The Mom at the PTO Meeting

MILFs

"Alright, I guess it's time to make my way over there.

I readied myself, leaving the office and heading to the PTO meeting. It was the first one I was invited to. Apparently, we were planning a huge fundraiser and bake sale for the school, and they wanted everyone's support. Normally I didn't give a rat's ass about this kind of thing, but it was for my daughter Alicia, so I guess I could see what this is.

I've never been the type to go to this kind of shit. Usually, it was kind of an obligation rather than of course, an actual decision on my own. But there was something thrilling, exciting, and fun about the idea of heading to this PTO meeting to meet some of the other parents.

It couldn't be too bad, right?

When I got there, I walked in, pushed my glasses up, and looked around. All of them seemed like your average parent, older, together with someone, and seemed to not want to be there even if someone paid them.

But there was one woman in the corner. She wore a sleek business suit, had her brown hair combed back in a tight bun, and seemed just as ready to leave as the rest of us.

There was also an empty seat there.

"Can I sit down?" I asked.

"Oh, sure! I guess I'm not the only single parent here," she said.

"Yeah, true," I told her.

I flushed, seeing her eyes linger over me. She then extended her hand.

"Alyssa," she said.

"Arnold," I replied.

She was probably the prettiest woman I've spoken to besides well... my late wife. Alyssa looked gorgeous, and when she looked into my eyes, she smiled.

"So, I guess you got roped into this too huh?"

"Yeah, cookies and fundraisers and such. I don't really have time to do this," I told her.

"Me neither. I can support, but I don't really want to waste my time doing these fundraisers," she said.

"Indeed. I run my own company, so this is not up my alley," I explained.

"You do? Oh, wow, that's so cool. I'm kind of climbing the ladder, so I'm definitely trying to get to that point," she told me.

"For sure."

We began talking, but I couldn't help but wonder if maybe, just maybe, this may turn into...something more. Something deeper. I couldn't help but marvel and think about that, especially given the instances that were happening.

For a long time, we stayed silent. The head of the PTO began blathering about how they were trying to make sales and such, but I couldn't help but feel my heart skip a beat as I looked over at Alyssa. She was gorgeous, and she seemed to have a wonderful head on her shoulders.

And I couldn't help but find that really attractive if I do say so myself.

The meeting was soon over, but then, Alyssa got up, looking at me.

"Well, that sucked," she said.

"Ugh, yeah. I could've just had this all emailed to me. but nooo," I told her.

"Right. Same here. Ugh, I just wanted a night off for once, and I had to go to this," she told me.

"Yeah, I feel that. My daughter is with her grandparents, so I finally had a little bit of freedom," I explained.

"I see. Well, if you want...you can come over to mine," she said.

She was older, but god she was attractive. I really was only here for my daughter, but honestly...I liked the idea of this.

"Sure, I wouldn't mind that," I said.

I could see the look in her eyes. A rampaging desire. Something she refused to admit until now. I wanted her to tell me a little bit more, and some of the other interesting aspects of herself, and as she got up, I saw a hint of her thighs against her skirt.

I licked my lips, realizing just how utterly beautiful she was.

I didn't want to get my hopes up though. The truth is, I felt like...if I did that, things would get a bit harder for me, but I kind of liked the idea behind it. Maybe I wanted to just take her and have my way with her right then and there.

But I also knew that I should take this slow.

We left the PTO building, and Alyssa turned to her car.

"Want to possibly meet at my place?"

"Sure, if that's okay with you," I told her.

She gave me something, flushing.

"My address. Let's link up," she said.

I pocketed it, nodding.

"Of course," I told her.

She winked, heading to the car, and as I looked downwards, seeing the address, I realized she wanted this as much as I did. And that's something that excited the fuck out of me.

Maybe it was the lack of action I've been getting, but I was more than ready to explore her body, to see what she had hidden underneath that business suit.

I then got to the car and drove to the location she gave me. it was a nice little place, and when I got to her one-story house, I pulled up. There was a tiny garden with little potters there. I saw that Alyssa made it home earlier.

I didn't know she was so sudden and forceful, inviting me home like this. I felt like...this was only going to get more and more interesting.

Not that I minded.

When I got to the door I knocked, and moments later she opened up.

"There you are Arnold," she said.

"Hey! I told you I'd be over," I teased.

"Course. I'm excited that you came," she said.

And as she said that, I don't know, something about that seemed very genuine to me.

"Well, I'm glad to be here," I told her.

She opened the door, letting me inside, and when I got in, I noticed how pretty the place was. It was beautiful if I did say so myself, and when she showed me in, I couldn't help but feel a little bit excited about this.

"Wow, you keep the place nice," I told her.

"Thanks. I try my best, what with all the hours that I do," she replied.

"Well, you certainly know how to not only work it, but also balance out your life. That's pretty admirable," I told her.

She laughed.

"It's not as cool as you think it is. Anyways, have a seat," she said.

She patted the area next to her, and I sat down. Alyssa then sighed.

"I'm just really glad that you're here you know. It's been a long time since I've actually...gone out with someone you know," she said.

"Really? I'm surprised. You're quite beautiful," I told her.

"Oh, thanks. It's just hard. Being a single mom, trying to keep everything together. I also haven't really found the right man for the job, especially with my little girl involved and all," she said.

I smirked, looking at her and smiling.

"Well, maybe you just need the right man for the job," I told her, reaching out and touching her thigh.

She turned to me, smirking.

"Really? And you think you're the perfect one for this?" she asked.

"I could very well be. I definitely have...a lot of interesting points if I do say so myself," I told her.

She looked me in the eyes, and then she nodded.

"Well thank you. I'm glad that I can interest you, even if only a little bit," she said.

"But of course. Anyways, I do want to say that you're quite the looker. And we're alone...right?" I asked her.

I didn't want a kid to come in while I was plowing their mom, that's for sure.

She then laughed.

"Yeah, don't worry, she's at her grandma's. I got a bit of a reprieve tonight," she said.

"Well, perhaps I can help you take care of that tension you've got. Looks like you have a lot," I told her.

"Oh, if you even knew," she teased.

I leaned forward, grabbing her chin, seeing that look in her eyes. She was gorgeous, and easily my type.

Before I knew it, my lips were on hers, enjoying the soft, subtle touch of her. She had softer lips than I expected, and there was something really nice about all of that. I looked at her as I did this, seeing her close her eyes, relishing in the touch of the kiss. I stayed like this with her, taking a moment to explore every part of her lips and beautiful body, before I moved back.

"You good?" I asked her.

"Amazing really. I didn't expect you to be so forward. I kind of like having a man in charge," she purred.

I liked being the man in charge of her. I quickly kissed her again, enjoying the touch of her body, and the little sounds that she made as I kissed her. There was something almost tantalizing, addicting, and needy about this, and as I kissed her, I felt that need for so much more, and I ached for it.

I grabbed her, pulling her smaller body into my arms, kissing her with a dire passion. Our tongues moved forward, enjoying the taste and feel of one another. And in truth, I couldn't help but enjoy everything that she gave to me, and the feelings that were brought forward.

She then pulled me closer, moving her body so that our hips ground against one another. I let out a small groan, feeling excited and needy. I wanted her, and as she pulled away, she smiled.

"Want to take this upstairs?" she asked.

"Sure.," I told her.

She smiled, grabbing my hand and bringing me upstairs. When we got in there, I moved her towards the bed, pushing her down, kissing her passionately.

It was a dream come true. Being able to savor and taste this woman, this different type of experience, it was all so damn perfect, that I didn't know how to even move away from it, but when she pulled away, she looked me in the eyes, giving me a teasing smile.

"I have something even more special for you tonight," she said.

"What do you mean?" I asked.

She gave me a small kiss, beaming.

"You'll see," she replied.

I started to flush, moving my hands against her body, touching her curves, feeling up every part of her. She let out a small gasp as I moved my hands upward, touching her breasts, and then she smirked.

"You have such a good touch, maybe we can...take this a little bit further," she purred.

That's exactly what I wanted. I wanted to feel her, to experience her, to touch her in every single way. I started to look into her eyes, and for a long time, I saw her look at me, a look of pure hunger growing between us.

Did she...want me as much as I wanted her? Perhaps that was the case. And even if she didn't say it outright, she definitely had a whole feeling that made me lose my mind.

Her hands reached up, touching me softly, looking at me in the eyes.

"Go on ahead," she said.

And that's what I did. Her body was still supple, even for being an older woman. There was a thrill that came with being with someone who was around my age, who had a similar history to me. Maybe that's why I was so gravitated toward her, and everything that she did.

I started to move my lips downward, kissing and teasing the flesh on her neck, and then, I saw her tense up, and for a long time, I started to feel her body just relax, taking in every part of me. I started to feel her body relax more and more, and as I reached up, touching her from under her jacket, feeling her breasts there, she let out a sigh.

"You have quite the hands there," she said.

"Thank you. I could say the same to you," I purred.

She smiled.

"You flatter me," she said.

I then slowly pulled off her jacket and shirt, watching as her eyes widen, and for a long time, I simply just basked in the feeling of this, enjoying her body, relishing her touch. I started to move my hands downward, cupping her breasts, touching them there, watching her slowly start to let out a small gasp, pushing her hands upwards, letting out the delicious sounds.

Fuck, I couldn't get enough of this. I began to pull off her bra, tossing it to the side. She laid there topless and beautiful, and I started to realize I was hungry for her.

It'd been so long since I had sex, and the fact that she laid there, looking at me with a small wink and smile, it was enough to drive me crazy, and it made me ache for her.

I moved my hands downwards, starting to touch the tips of her breasts. She let out a small moan, tensing up, and then, I began to move my tongue towards her nipple, taking it between my lips, suckling on it while I flicked my tongue over her. She let out a low groan, holding me there as I started to move and explore her, enjoying the sounds that she made as I continued to experience her.

The fact that she was here, relishing the taste of me, it was all just...so damn perfect and so good, that I couldn't help but wonder just what else she had planned for me next.

I continued to move my hands, teasing her other nipple against my fingers, pressing my fingers slightly, watching as her eyes widened, and the sounds that she made driving me to the point of madness.

But as I finished, she looked up at me, and I noticed something different in her eyes.

A hunger.

Before I knew it, she flipped me over, leaving me down on the bed. I looked at her, and she had a smirk on her face.

"Told you I had something special planned," she said.

"What do you—"

Before I knew it, her lips were on mine, a domineering kiss driving me to the point of madness. She continued to kiss me, and for a long time, I eagerly accepted it. Then, she pulled back, touching my face.

"You look so cute when you sit there, practically begging for more. I take it you didn't realize that I like to be in control, and sometimes…I just like to have a little bit of fun taking over, seeing you lose your mind like this," she said.

I gulped. I realized I was in bed with a woman who was secretly a dom. She pretended to be all innocent, and just your average horny MILF.

But she wasn't.

She quickly pulled off my shirt, moving her hands, teasing my pecs, moving towards the tip of my nipples. She then grazed her fingers, causing a sudden rush of excitement to shift through my body.

"Holy shit," I told her.

"What's the matter? You struggling to hold back? Trying not to lose control?" she teased.

"Yeah," I said.

"Well don't worry, I want you to lose control. I like seeing men come undone like this," she said.

She teased my nipples once again, making me suddenly relish the pleasure, enjoying the feel of this as she did this. She continued to tease every part of me, and as I realized the fact that I was with a secret femdom, I kind of liked it.

I thought she would just be your average little innocent woman, but this hit different, not necessarily in a bad way. In fact, it…it felt good.

I felt her hands tease my nipples, making me suddenly shiver and push forward, moaning in pleasure at the feeling of this. I started to look at her, seeing the excitement in her eyes as she did this.

"There you go. Good boy. Look at you, all coming undone like this. This is my favorite type of guy. The kind that lets me have pure control, that lets me touch and tease them fully and lets me watch them slowly come undone with every little touch," she said.

"Ahh yes," I told her. I thrust upward, watching her smile as she slowly moved her hands downward. She teased the very tip of my cock from within my pants.

That's when I jolted forward. I couldn't take it. I felt like she was just going to completely tease me for the rest of the session, till I came.

"Ahh please," I said.

"Please what?" she teased.

I looked at Alyssa, who tried to play stupid, but I knew that she knew exactly what I needed.

"Please...tease me. Let me breathe," I told her. I knew that my cock was practically begging for me to be let loose. She looked at me, smiling.

"There we go. All I wanted to hear from you. You're very easy to tease and work with, that's something that I very much enjoy from you," she said.

"Yes," I purred.

She then smiled, moving downward, teasing me. I shivered, moaning slightly.

"What was that? I didn't hear you?" she said.

Fuck, she really did play hard to get. I sat there, holding the edge of the bed, feeling her hands continue to move with each and every single touch.

"Please, just...let me out," I told her.

"Alright then," she said.

She undid the button on my pants, and then the fly, pulling them and my boxers off. My cock sprang out, and she barely touched it, causing me to let out a small gasp, holding the bed.

"Wow, you're really hard already. How cute. But I kind of want to tease a little bit more," she said.

"What do you plan on—"

As I said that, she got up, pulling off her skirt and panties, moving herself so that she straddled my head. She rested there, making me suddenly shiver with delight, enjoying the feeling of this as I continued to gasp, tasting all of her. She shoved her pussy into my face, and I eagerly tasted it all.

"There we go. Good boy. Now that you've satisfied me, maybe I'll do more than touch you. Or maybe I'll wait till you can make me cum," she said.

Hearing those words was such a turn-on to me. I was already losing my damn mind, and I couldn't help but feel it start to make me feel like I was at my wit's end. I started to thrust my body upward, feeling every part of this drive me to the brink.

"Fuck," I said under her.

She smiled, shoving her pussy further towards my face. I explored, savoring the taste, sticking my tongue against her entrance, fucking her restlessly with my tongue. As I did that, she held the bed, crying out loud, enjoying the feeling of this.

She continued to shove her pussy into my face, forcing me to eat her out. I enjoyed every moment of this, savoring the taste, the feeling, and everything that came from it. The sounds that she made, including the way that she tried to hold back her own moans, was enough to drive me crazy too. I looked at her, and she simply smiled.

"There we go," she said to me. I looked at her, knowing that this was indeed what she wanted, and it was something that I desired too.

I continued to satisfy her, enjoying the little sounds. When I moved my tongue upward, hitting that one part of her, I suddenly felt her body shiver, holding herself down. I struggled to breathe, but at the same time, I savored it, hearing the delicious sounds that came out of her.

"Fuck!" she said.

She then let out a series of cries, cumming, and smearing my face with her juices. She was filthy, and I loved it. She then finished, and she looked over at me, smiling.

"There we go," she said to me.

"Ahh," I said out loud as she moved away from me. I would kill to have her smother my face completely once again, but she stopped herself, looking me in the eyes.

"Well, what did I tell you? Pretty good huh?" she said.

"Yes. I want more," I told her.

She then laughed.

"Well, why don't I give you a little treat then," she said.

She then moved herself so that she was right over my cock. She touched it, barely letting her fingers drape there, and suddenly, I let out a small groan, completely enamored in the feeling that this gave me. She then laughed, seeing me slowly come apart.

"Look at you. So turned on that you can't even think straight. How pathetic," she said.

"Yes, I'm pathetic. I just want you," I told her.

That probably sounded so lame, but I couldn't stop thinking about this, and how amazing this felt. I looked into her eyes, seeing the look of pure desire there. She soon moved herself so that she was right up against my cock, letting her hands touch the tip of it, and then grabbing the shaft, jerking it slightly.

I looked at her, feeling completely lost in the touch that I felt. She smiled, jerking me right then and there, watching me with widened, expectant eyes.

"You're not allowed to cum yet," she said to me.

"Okay," I told her, cringing as I felt her hand grab my hard dick, keeping me right then and there. She continued to jerk me slightly, watching my eyes practically roll to the back of my head.

Then, I felt her lips. I suddenly realized that she knew exactly how to drive me to the edge. She soon moved her lips so that she was right against the tip of my body, and then, before I knew it, she pushed her lips to the tip, sucking on it before taking me downward. She let her tongue move forwards, getting from the underside over to the tip of my dick. I watched with a rapturous look, seeing her there, holding me there. I felt like I was at the mercy of her touches, and there was something shocking, but such a turn-on surrounding it.

"Yes," I said.

"What's that?"

"Please...more," I told her.

She then giggled, touching me right then and there, looking me in the eyes as she did it.

"Really now. What is it that you want then?" she said.

She then took her mouth and pushed downwards, getting about halfway. She stuck her tongue out, pushing against the underside. I let out a small groan, holding there. She continued bobbing her head up and down, leaving me a fucking mess right there in front of her.

I was completely enamored in the touch of this, aching for more, but also knowing damn well that she could just stop this at any time, and just make me lose it all right then and there.

I was so close already, and when her fingers moved towards my balls, touching there slightly, I felt my eyes practically loll to the back of my head. I was about to lose it, shivering there as I let out a small groan.

"Fuck," I told her.

"What's the matter?" she said.

I was about to cum. But I didn't want to cum.

"I can stop right now, and you can cum inside me. You want that, don't you?" she said.

"Yes," I whispered.

"What was that?" I can't hear you," she said.

This fucking tease. She was doing this to make me lose it. Then I spoke, realizing that I was at her mercy.

"Please. Let me cum," I said right then and there.

She giggled.

"Fine, I'll let you cum. But I'm on top," she said.

Before I could say anything else, she slowly slid herself down against me, holding me there. Her pussy felt so warm and tight that I relished the feel of it. I looked at her, seeing her smile there.

"There you go. Now just relax. I'll take great care of you," she purred.

And I knew that she would. She began to move up and down, letting her pussy completely smother all of my senses, making me lose my mind right then and there. I grabbed her, and I held onto her as she started to move her hips up and down into that one sort of style, making me lose all semblance of reality, completely mesmerized by the feeling of this.

"Holy shit," I told her.

"Yes? What is it?" she said.

"I can't...I can't hold back. Please let me c um," I said.

I felt a little pathetic for begging, but her pussy was so good. I reached up, touching her tits, feeling her let out a small moan of surprise as she started to move against me.

"There we go. Good boy. I want to hear you beg for it though," she said.

"Please, let me cum," I said, realizing how pathetic I probably sounded. But in truth, I didn't care anymore. I ached for her, I needed her, and then, after a few more thrusts, she pushed in, making me lose my mind.

I then came hard, feeling myself just lose it there. I reached out, rubbed her clit, and then, she let out a small gasp, cumming as well as I finished off with her. I was a mess, completely lost in the touch of her pussy, and I knew that she liked this too.

She finished, finally moving off of me, looking me in the eyes as she smiled.

"Damn," she said to me.

"What's up?" I said.

"It's been a while since a man kept up with me like that. I'm going to be honest, most of them can't handle a woman who...likes to be in charge," she said to me.

I flushed, realizing that she saw me as something more, something different. I mean, it wasn't what I was used to, but I tried my best to kind of accept it.

"I mean, I like to make things fun, whatever they may end up being," I told her.

"True. Anyways, you were a fun lay, and I'm glad I went to that PTO meeting," Alyssa teased.

I reached out, touched her hair, and looked her in the eyes. I never thought that I would nab a girl who preferred to be dominant. In a strange way, that was so fucking hot to me.

"You know, I kind of like that you're dominant. It's a bit different if I do say so myself," I told her.

"Course it is. That's why I struggle to meet new guys. A lot of them just see me as someone that they can top and take control of. But honestly...I like it when I can have my own little fun you know," she said.

"It's different, that's for sure, but I kind of like it," I told her.

"I figured you would. Thank you for that though Arnold. You really are the first guy I've met who just gets it, and I like that," she said.

I blushed. I'm glad that I could be an interesting person to her, and someone that she could trust as well. I reached out and looked her in the eyes as I touched her slightly, holding my hand there.

"I'm really glad that I can make you feel good," I told her.

"I feel the same way too," she replied.

I leaned in, giving her a long, passionate kiss as we stayed like this, enjoying the touch of one another. There was something exciting about this, and for a long time, I simply stayed like this, enjoying the soft touch of her lips. Then, she pulled back, looking me in the eyes slightly.

"So, do you want to...maybe go out on a date or something?" she asked me.

I was surprised that she wanted to do that. I mean, I couldn't really say no, but I also was shocked that this was something that she wanted as well.

"Sure, if that's what you desire?" I asked her.

"Yes, it sure as shit is. I really want that," she told me.

I beamed, reaching out and touching her cheek, looking into her eyes and smiling.

"Well, I'm glad that I can enjoy this with you then. I'm sure it'll be good for both of us," I told her.

She beamed.

"It sure will be. And I'm glad that you get it. I like being a dominant woman in the bedroom, even though usually...I tend to be more submissive outside of the bedroom," she said.

"Well it's different, but not something that I can't get used to," I told her.

She smiled.

"Thanks, Arnold. It's weird, you're like the first guy I've fucked who gets it. Most of them don't understand, and I like that a lot about you," she said.

"Well I try to, and I'm glad that I'm someone who you can rely on," I told her.

She beamed, giving me one last kiss.

And that's how I ended up hooking up with a MILF who was similar to me, and someone at the PTO meeting. This was fun, and something I would do again in a heartbeat. I felt good, happy, and ready for action next time. I knew that Alyssa was fun, and she was different, and I knew for a fact that she was someone that would be remembered in my head, and someone that I could never forget, no matter what happened between us next, and how things went from here.

Her Strange Fetish

Feet, BDSM, Tickle

"What was it that you wanted to talk about?" my dom boyfriend Glen asked.

I flushed. I wanted to try it, especially since it was something that I saw.

"Say glen, have you ever thought about well…. Feet stuff?" I asked him.

He looked at me, slightly surprised by my words.

"Can't say I have," he said.

"Well, it's just…it's something that I wanted to try during our next play session. I saw it and figured it…it might be kind of fun," I told him.

I figured that this may be something weird to talk about, but maybe Glen would get it. We have talked about what we want to try and like before. Feet was never something on the table though.

But it was because I found a video a couple of days ago. It was a woman, fully clothed, but the fetish was tickling. She ended up orgasming after that happened. When I saw it, I thought that it was the hottest shit, but I had no idea how to convince Glenn that it was okay to try it.

"Are you sure that you want to try it?" Glen asked.

"Yeah, I do. I figured it would be kind of weird. Plus, I mean, you're always commenting how nice my feet look. Maybe it might be something you could enjoy too," I told him.

He looked at me, slightly surprised by this, but then, he nodded.

"Are you sure about this?" he asked me.

"Yeah, positive Glen. Let's...try something new," I told him.

I figured this would be a little bit weird for us, but Glen took a moment to process it. He took a deep breath and then nodded.

"Yeah, we can try that next time," he said.

I beamed, excited to experience this.

"I'm sure we'll both love it," I told him.

"I think so too," he said to me.

So that's what we agreed on. In our next play session, we would try the feet and the tickling stuff. I felt excited to explore this. Because maybe it would be something new that I could enjoy.

It wasn't the first time I'd been into weird fetishes of course. I loved being degraded, and I loved being put into embarrassing positions. Maybe this foot thing was just the right step forward.

That night, I sat on the bed, waiting for him to come home. He told me to get on the bed and get ready. I braced myself, wearing a sheer pair of panties and a sheer bra that showed the outline of my rosy pink nipples. I flushed thinking about this.

Would he enjoy it? Or would this be another fetish that we'd toss to the side because we both ended up hating it? Honestly, I didn't know for sure, but I wanted to believe that there may be a chance for both of us to explore this, enjoy one another, and have a good time.

Then, I heard the sound of the door unlock. I moved towards the doorway, seeing Glenn there. He was dressed in a pair of tight leather pants, and he looked me over, smiling.

"There you are. Been waiting a while?"

"No Master. I was just...getting ready," I said.

"I see. Say my pet, there's something I've been curious about," he said.

"What do you mean?" I asked. I didn't know how he would respond to this, but I figured it would be a fun little thing.

He looked at me, and then down at my feet. I had painted them a pretty color to add to the experience.

"Your feet look really nice," he said.

"Thank you, Master," I said.

He then reached up, touching them, caressing them. It sent a jolt through my body, causing me to flush, letting out a small gasp and moan of pleasure.

"What's the matter? You like it when I touch your feet?" he asked.

"Yes," I said.

"Well tell you what, why don't you get comfortable, and Master can service these feet as much as you'd like," he said to me.

I looked at Glenn, nodding.

"Alright," I said.

I laid down on the bed, noticing that his hands moved to my arms, putting them in the restraints that we had. What did he have planned next? He looked over at my feet, letting his hands barely touch against the tips of them, caressing downward, watching as I let out a small moan of pleasure at the touch.

"Damn, turned on already?" he teased.

"It feels...nice," I told him.

"Well...Master can give you a nice little foot massage. And then a little bit of a punishment too after we're done," he purred right up in my ear, licking against the edge.

The way his voice came off right then and there made me shiver with delight, moaning in response as I started to feel my whole body react to his touch. I was completely lost in this, amazed at how nice this felt, and how this just...made me want more.

"Yes. I'd really like that."

"Yes, what?"

"Yes, Master," I breathed out, feeling my breath hitch as he started licking and caressing down my neck, touching and teasing every part of me, making me lose control, moaning in response, enjoying the touch of his hands as he continued touching me.

Even just the littlest of touches was enough to turn me the fuck on, and as he moved his hands down, just barely touching my body, I felt like I was on the very edge. I loved everything about this, feeling the enjoyment of it as I continued to feel his hands move further downward, past my pussy and thighs, going for what he had his attention on first.

My feet.

I knew that deep down glen also had a foot fetish, but he was quiet about it. At least, until now that is. He continued to touch the edges of my feet, tickling them slightly.

I suddenly tensed up, curling them, feeling my whole body jolt forward. I stayed against the bindings, but I let out a small gasp of pleasure, feeling him tickle my feet.

"Holy shit," I said.

"What's the matter there? You liking it?" Glenn said, touching my feet once more.

I quickly laid there, experiencing the pleasure that came from this. It was like a surge of energy, and of need.

"Ahh yes!" I told him, curling my toes as he continued to let his hands crawl against the tips of my feet, resting on the soles. He got to the back of my foot, and with just one little touch, I practically jolted forward, crying out in pleasure as he did this.

There was something about the way this man just touched my feet, making me lose my goddamn mind, experiencing the fun and loss of control as he did this. I loved it, and as he continued to touch me there, holding me, I suddenly started to tense up, moaning out loud.

"You good?" he said to me.

"Amazing," I finally breathed out. but that was an understatement.

I didn't expect to get off to the feeling of my feet being tickled. But then he got in between the toes, moving against the underside of my big toe, letting his tongue roll out, touching the very edges.

I cried out, moaning out loud, enjoying his hands and lips as he continued to suckle and tease every part of my toes. It was like I was experiencing a whole new world, a world of feet that of course was something that I enjoyed far more than I expected. I started to feel his hands move upward, tickling the underside of the front of my feet as he sucked on my toes, and I cried out, holding myself there as I felt the pleasure from being tickled just completely destroy me.

It was a weird fetish, and it wasn't something that most people were into, but seeing his hands there, touching and teasing every part of me, it was just...enough to drive me insane. I continued to hold onto the edge, tensing up as I cried out, moaning out loud as I felt like I was on the very edge.

It was then when, moments later, he then moved to the sides of my feet, teasing there with his tongue. When he did that, I suddenly held onto him, moaning out loud as I struggled to hold back. But it wasn't like there was much I could do, and not much to say. I simply just felt the feeling of losing control hit me, making me shiver with delight, crying in pleasure, and loving everything about this.

He continued to service my feet, no matter how dirty and gross they got. There was something so nice about it, especially since Glenn seemed to develop this fetish as he went along too.

Then, he pulled away, looking at my dainty, soft feet there. He touched the middle part of them, massaging my feet, and it was enough to make me scream out once again, holding onto it, and then, feeling my body get so close to orgasm. As soon as he touched it though, he stopped, looking me in the eyes as he smiled.

"You good?" he asked me.

"Amazing," I told him.

"Good. I like seeing you turned on," he told me.

"I love...I love what you keep doing to my feet, Master," I cried out.

"Of course you do. You're a little degenerate who gets off to feet. How nasty," he said.

He then moved toward the nightstand, grabbing something. As he did that, he came back over, resting the item against my feet. It was a small little feather tickler, and when I felt it there, I grimaced, biting my lip as I felt it.

"Holy shit," I told myself.

"You okay?"

"Yes," I said.

He let the tickler touch the very tip of my feet, making my toes curl, and my body suddenly lost all semblance of control. I began to feel my body suddenly relax, emerging deep into the bowels of pleasure as I felt it all take over me. His hands moved downwards, getting to the middle of my feet, moving there. I cried out, grabbing the chains once again, completely lost in the touch. I felt my body tense up, the pleasure driving me crazy. I didn't expect just mere tickling to drive me crazy, but the more he did it, even the smallest of touches, was enough to make me hold my tongue, cry out, and lose my mind.

He then pressed there once again, and suddenly, I felt the overwhelming sensation of pleasure as I felt my orgasm hit me hard, causing me to tense up, cry out loud, and then cum hard against him.

He then moved his hands away, looking at me as I laid there, completely immersed in the pleasure.

"Looks like you really do get off to tickling and your feet. I never expected this from you," he said.

"Ahh, yes," I told him.

He then moved his hands upward, touching the sides of my body. He began to tickle me there, making me hold my tongue, cry out, and tense up once again.

I was very ticklish. I didn't expect to get off to mere tickling like this, but it was hot to say the least, and I ached for more. His hands moved against me, tickling my sides, making me laugh out loud.

"Yes, yes"! I screamed, holding myself there, completely immersed in it all, the pleasure driving me mad. He continued to tease me, watching my eyes widen with pleasure and desire, the excitement growing within me. I began to feel my insides tense up, and I was turned on by tickling.

I didn't know this was a legitimate fetish until he did this just now. It was like I discovered something new and raw, utterly amazing, and with every single tickling touch, I felt my body jerk forward, the lurking feeling of being tickled and at this man's mercy just becoming an arousing moment for me.

For a few moments, I felt his hands skirt up and down, causing me to lose my mind. I loved being a sub to this type of feeling. Being a little bitch to my Master as he tickled me. but then, just as I was about to cum again, he stopped, looking at me.

"I have a little proposition for you," he said.

"What is it?" I asked.

"If you can last being tickled while I fuck you to the point where I cum, I'll let you get off with a tickle orgasm," he said.

I flushed. He was having a blast with this.

"So, I have to last as long as I can?"

"Correct. A test of endurance. For both of us," he purred.

I liked the sound of this. But it would be a challenge, considering how good he was at holding back to the point where I doubted that he would just get overtaken.

"Please. Please fuck me," I said.

I didn't mean to sound so needy, but my whole body craved it. I saw him smile, and then, I expected him to just plunge into my pussy.

"Not just yet. I didn't tell you where I was going to fuck you yet," he said.

What did he mean by—"

As soon as I thought that he then moved a lubed finger towards my pucker, which stood there, open for the taking. I flushed, tensing up, crying out as I felt the finger move in, teasing me right then and there. He began to press the fingers deep within me, making me suddenly lose my mind, holding me there as I tensed up, feeling the need for more.

More...please," I said.

I was so turned on, but I knew that he wouldn't let me get off with just that. He soon added a second finger, pushing all the way into me, causing me to tense up, suddenly crying out loud, completely lost in the pleasure of it. He pushed the two fingers in, and then grabbed my foot, teasing it against his tongue.

I howled, begging for him to just fuck me right then and there. I didn't know how long I could last with all of this, and he seemed to get a thrill from this. Maybe that's what he was trying to go for. To watch me completely lose myself, and beg for more.

"What, you want my cock already?"

"Yes, please," I said.

He then tickled my feet, which caused me to scream out, holding onto the bindings, looking at him. I was at the mercy of this man's touch, and I loved every goddamn minute of it.

"Well since you asked so nicely, perhaps I could satisfy those desires. But I don't know, you seem to be almost too much fun to be with," he said to me.

"Ahh, please," I told him.

"Please, what?"

"Please give me your cock. I beg you," I said.

I normally wasn't the begging type, but I was already at my fucking limit. He smiled, pushing me back even further so that my feet were near my head. He then lubed up his cock, spreading my cheeks apart, and then slid himself all the way inside of me. I shivered, feeling it all hit me at once, making me suddenly lose control, completely aching for him, knowing that he enjoyed this as much as I did.

After a brief moment, he stayed there, looking me in the eyes, and for a long time, we simply stayed like this. Then, he began to move, and I suddenly felt that urge, that need, and that desire. But I was so close already. However, I didn't want to cum yet.

I knew that I wouldn't get off fully if I came right then and there. I started to look at him, seeing the smile on his face as he started to move his cock in and out, completely breaching me. I laid there, taking all of this, when suddenly, he grabbed my foot, rubbing it.

That bastard! He was trying to tease me on purpose! To make sure that I'd lose it right then and there. He was totally trying to see me lose my mind, and it was then when, after a few more thrusts, he then pushed all the way in.

"Fuck, you're so tight. I can't wait to get you off with your favorite move," he said.

I laid there, engulfed in pleasure, enjoying the touch of this, completely losing every part of my mind as he continued.

He pushed in deep, holding me there as he groaned, spilling himself all the way inside of me, watching my eyes widen as he filled up my hole. He finished up, pushing out, looking at me there. I was in a compromising position, my whole body just completely lost in the pleasure of this, and when he looked at me, he smiled.

"There we go," he said.

"What do you…mean," I asked him.

"I see you right there. You seem to be a good girl. But maybe I just…want to fill you up completely. And then tickle you, making you spill out all of the cum that you have inside. How about that," he said.

He touched me, teasing me there, making me suddenly gasp with pleasure. Was he really going to put it inside me again? Or was he just messing with me? His touches moved downward, getting to that area between my legs where my legs met my crotch. He pressed against there, making me suddenly huff with surprise, completely enraptured in the feeling of this.

"What do you say? You want to be filled up by me first in both your holes, and then tickled to orgasm?" he asked, touching me slightly with his fingers.

I liked the idea of it, but was he ready to do that again? I looked at him, and after he wiped himself down, he smiled.

"I'm waiting," he said.

"Yes," I finally said, completely lost in the feeling of this.

"Yes, what? I can't hear you," he teased.

That bastard! But then I sighed.

"Yes. Please fill up my holes, Master. I need it," I told him.

I didn't expect to sound like such a needy bitch, but I was already lost in the pleasure, in the fun, and lost in the feelings that this gave to me. He looked at me, resting his fingers against my pussy.

"Maybe I should tease you further too. Tickle you to the point of orgasm, but not let you have it. How does that sound?"

I wanted to refuse, but then, before I knew it, his hands moved upward, teasing the very edge of my armpits. As he did this, his hand moved downward, touching and exploring me. He looked me dead in the eyes as I laid there, completely lost in the pleasure that Glenn gave to me. the little touches set me on fire, and I knew that when I did finally orgasm again, I would completely lose it, and that's something that excited me too.

He pumped his fingers in and out, holding me there, watching as my eyes started to widen, completely lost in the feeling of this. He then moved his fingers upward, moving right up against my G-spot. He teased there, watching as I widened my eyes, holding him there as I continued to shiver, cry out with pleasure, and lose my mind and body.

Every part of me wanted more of this, and everything craved the touch of him. He continued this tease, these amazing feelings of pleasure, driving me mad, and it was then when, after a few more moments, he pulled away, and I looked at him with annoyance. But then, he tickled me while he tickled my armpits. He moved his hands to my clit, tapping and teasing there, watching as my eyes practically rolled to the back of my head, holding everything still there as I continued to experience him. I knew that he was doing all of this on purpose, to get me so close that I would lose my mind, but it was then when, after a few more moments, a few more thrusts, I was right at my limit.

But like he said, he pulled away, his fingers sopping wet from my aching need.

"Damn girl, you really want this don't you?" he said.

"Yes. Please. Give it to me," I said. I didn't expect begging to cum would be the one thing that I desired, but I knew for a fact that he had me in the palm of his hand, watching me, seeing the way that I reacted to everything. He then moved back, spreading me apart, looking at me there.

"You're so cute, hun. I can't wait to watch you squirm in response to what I have in store for you," he said.

Before I could say anything more, he spread my legs far apart, sliding all the way in. He held me there, but I already let out a garbled series of sounds, completely lost in the feeling of this, and I knew that he enjoyed this too. He started to push himself in deep, watching my eyes widen, and my whole body completely lose it. I started to feel like I was so close to my limit that I didn't know what would happen next. After a few more moments, and a few more thrusts, I started tensing up. I knew that I was at the end, at the limit, but he stopped me.

He pushed upward, narrowly avoiding that spot, and then, he let out a groan. A series of small spurts of cum filled me up completely, making me slowly lose my mind. Everything about this just felt so damn good, that I couldn't get enough of it. I looked at him as he made his last couple of thrusts, pushing away from me, seeing the cum that was there as it spurted out of my holes.

"Beautiful," he said.

I was so horny still. I needed a release. I looked at him, a look of pure need on my face.

"Right, you want this, don't you?"

"Yes. I need to cum. Please. I'm so close," I said, moving my hands there.

"Well, in that case, I'm going to make it an orgasm that you won't forget," he told me.

What else could he possibly do here? What else could he...do to make me lose my mind? But then, he grabbed a couple of ticklers, moving toward where my armpits were.

Oh, so this was what he had planned for me. He rested the feather tickler gently against me, looking at me, seeing the way that I seemed so passive because I was so needy. I begged for a release because I didn't know how much more of this I could take, or even what I could do anymore.

He smiled, watching me squirm. He then moved his hands upward, with the feather tickler. He got behind my head, resting them on my armpits.

"Then cum," he said.

He began dragging them there, and I let out a small moan. I started to feel my whole body begin to lose control, squirming about, and moaning. I pushed my legs together, the cum spilling out of me a little bit as I did so. I let out a small moan, suddenly feeling like I was at my limit. After a few more moments, he made his hands move a little bit faster, watching me tense up and cry out loud.

"Fuck," I said.

I knew that I couldn't hold back. But then he dug it deep into the crevice of my armpit, and then, as he did this, I suddenly moaned, holding myself there, tensing up as I felt the force of my orgasm hit me slightly. I looked at him, crying out loud, feeling my body tense up, my head spin, and my body move forward.

But what I didn't expect, was what else came out. there was something that came out of my pussy, spreading all around and creating a wet spot on the bed.

Holy shit. I squirted. I started to moan once again, feeling the high of my orgasm hit me hard, and he continued, watching me shiver, cry out with delight, and it was then after a few more moments, I suddenly started to tense up, feeling my whole body shiver, and then, I came hard once again, feeling the effects of this as he continued to tickle me.

It was like relentless feelings of pleasure, of orgasm, and of a feeling that was only going to drive me more and more to the limit. He pressed it there, and then, I screamed out, cumming hard, feeling like I was going insane.

After my fourth orgasm, he then stopped, pulling away to finally give me a moment of reprieve. I sat there, feeling filthy, but also completely satisfied in ways I didn't expect to feel. He looked at me as I smiled at him, happy and satisfied.

"Thank you," I told him.

"For what?"

"For...that. It's not every day I can admit my feelings about fetishes and not be seen as fucking weird," I told him.

He giggled.

"Well, you are weird, but you're my weirdo," he said.

"Thank you," I told him.

He leaned in, giving me a passionate kiss. We stayed like that, making out. he then undid the bindings, and I wrapped my arms around Glenn, my Master, and someone who seemed to understand my feelings and kinds. It's not every day that I got to experience something like this, and I felt really good about it.

After we kissed for a bit, he pulled back, looking at me.

"So how did you like it? Was I good enough?" he asked me.

"Yeah, it was amazing," I told him.

"Good. I'm glad that I can make you feel good," he told me.

I was glad about that too. I flushed though, and he looked at me with a bit of concern.

"Something the matter?" he asked.

"No, I'm just really happy that you gave me this chance. I feel a lot better," I told him.

"Yeah, I'm glad that you could trust me with this. Honestly, I think you helped unlock a foot fetish in me as well. I'm really just...glad that you're here with me," he said to me.

"I'm very glad too," I told him.

He gave me a long, passionate kiss, and I kissed him back, enjoying the touch of our lips. We stayed like this, kissing fervently for a little bit before he pulled away, smelling me.

"I think it's time for you and me to have a shower," he said.

"Yeah, I definitely feel that," I told him.

He reached out, taking my hand and squeezing it.

"And don't worry, you don't have to tell anyone about this. It'll be our little secret," he said.

I smiled.

"Yeah, it sure as shit will be our little secret," I told him.

"I'm sure that once we have everything sorted out, you'll be able to really experience the fun and kink of life, and I know that you will enjoy this more and more too," he said.

I beamed.

"Yeah, I do feel like it opened the door to something inside of me, something that I didn't expect to feel," I told him.

"Well, I'm glad that you're able to really express yourself, and feel good about it too," he replied.

"I'm really glad too. I'm just glad that...I could try this out in a place with someone who gets it. So, thanks babe," I told him.

"No problem," he replied.

He gave me a long, passionate kiss, and we stayed like this for a long period of time, just kissing and touching one another. I relished in this, and for a long time, I simply just experienced the moment, completely in awe at how good I felt. Everything just...really felt amazing. I was glad to have this, and then, as he looked at me, he smiled.

"And don't worry, I won't expose your secret to anyone. We can keep the feet and tickling between us," he said with a smirk.

I blushed but nodded.

"Thanks, babe. I do appreciate it. It's weird to really feel this way, but I'm glad that you're here with me," I told him.

"I'm glad too. And I'm glad that we can experience this together," he told me.

I smiled too.

We went to go take a shower, and I felt really good. Exhausted, but fucking good. I realized as I showered that I experienced something different, something completely fun, and I enjoyed every second of it. I wanted to feel more, and I knew that he did too.

But it was good to finally learn what I was into kind of, to really experience everything that I wanted to with it. I knew that it was different from what I was used to, and it probably was a bit of a weird kink for some people. But the fact that I had a partner who at least kind of understood this was...nice to say the least. And I felt like I was definitely happier too. There was a feeling of happiness, of settlement, and I knew that no matter what, we were in this together, and he would understand me, no matter what kinds of weird kinks I'd bring to the table next.

And that made me happy, made me feel good, and made me realize just how much he mattered to me.

The Cop's Newfound Fun

BDSM Roleplay

I didn't think that I'd take the demotion so terribly.

But I ended up feeling like a loser the moment I saw the email. They were making the department smaller, so the rookie cops that had been mostly on the sidelines were now demoted to grunt work at HQ.

It sucked. I missed driving around looking for people who needed help and arresting bad people.

Which was why I quit the force shortly after. It was totally my decision, unlike what my boss said to me.

The truth was, I wanted to explore new horizons, and see what other kinds of lives there were out there.

But I did miss the idea of roleplaying the scenarios, which was what made me seek out roleplay. I wanted to roleplay the high of being a cop once more, but I also...I also just wanted the sexual release from it.

And that's when I met Tyra.

Tyra was a former dominatrix, but now did mostly house calls as both a dom and a sub. When we met u, at first, I was a little bit nervous, but she ended up showing me the fun that came with my fetishes and fantasies. Of course, it was strictly casual, but Tyra really did help me with release.

That's when I prompted the question to her.

"Anything you want?" she asked, her darker skin a perfect contrast to the perfectly white sheets. Her lips curled into that of a wry smile as her dark brown eyes looked into my bluish-grey ones.

"Yeah, I was thinking…oh fuck I don't want to make it weird for either of us," I told her.

"If you have something that you want, you shouldn't be afraid to ask you know," she said.

"No, it's just…I'm sorry," I said.

She leaned forward, touching my face and looking into my eyes.

"You pay for this, if there is something that you want, now is the time to tell me," she pointed out.

She was right, even if I didn't want to admit it.

"It's more just like…I want to try out roleplay. I used to be a cop before I went into investing," I explained.

"Oh, that explains that feeling I got from you. I got the vibe that you were a cop or a nonpracticing one," she said.

"Well, I don't practice anymore for uh…reasons. But yeah, I kind of want to try new things," I told her.

"So, what you thinking? Anything in particular you want to try?" she asked me.

I flushed. I then nodded.

"Yeah, I want to roleplay being a cop, and punishing the criminal," I said.

"That sounds like fun," she said.

"Okay, so it's not weird then. Thank fuck," I told her.

She reached forward, touching my arm and looking at me.

"Honey, I will tell you if something is weird. And you're not weird," she said.

"Thanks," I replied with a smile.

I then grabbed her arms, pushing her down onto the ground.

"So, I heard that you were a naughty girl," I said.

I pushed my hands behind her back, and she moaned.

"Yes, I've been a VERY naughty girl," she said.

The way she said that had me going. There was a thrill of being in control, of being in charge, but also keeping this to a strictly bedroom setting. It was nice knowing that no matter what, we could explore one another, and enjoy each other's touch.

I trusted her, and I'm sure that she trusted me too.

I then pulled her upward, my lips right near her ear.

"So, you willing to be my little pet? I can make those naughty problems go away if you choose?" I offered.

"Ahh, yes," she said.

The way the words came out of her mouth was enough to drive me insane. I was so fucking hot and bothered by the words she uttered that I couldn't get enough.

"There we go. Now get to the wall," I said.

Tyra had a small wall for play, with two rings there. When she got there, I grabbed her arms, attaching them to the cuffs that were there. She then turned to me, a beaming grin on her face.

"So, Officer, what is my punishment?" she asked.

"Your punishment is quite deep, and I'm going to make sure you'll be feeling it...well into tomorrow," I told her. I reached forward, grabbing her butt, squeezing it, watching as she let out a small cry, pressing forward.

This was a whole lot of fun. I started to touch her, lightly patting the side.

"So, I caught you trying to escape my clutches. You think I, an Officer would let you go that easily?" I asked.

"N-no Officer, but I've been very bad," she said.

"Really now, show me how bad you've been. Tell me what you've been doing," I said.

She let out a small groan, and then, she spoke.

"I've been...touching myself without your permission, and I've been hiding that from you," she said.

I reached down, rubbing her there, causing her to let out a small moan of surprise, thrusting her hips up.

"What a naughty girl, getting off without permission. What should I do with you then…. I said to her.

"Everything," she said.

"You're so horny and desperate. Perhaps I'll make your juicy butt a little more marked up. I do have some toys that I'd love to use on you," I said to her.

"Yes, Officer, use all the toys that you want to on me. I'm your little slut, the one that you can count on, no matter what," she said.

I laughed, touching her backside and feeling her flinch slightly at the touch of my hands.

"You're so on edge already though…perhaps you've been…savoring this moment, waiting for me to take this seriously?" I said.

"Ahh yes. I want this. I'm…slowly losing my mind," I heard her say.

And that was a mutual feeling, that's for sure. I loved being in control, the power this bred. I moved my hand against her soft skin, watching her slowly gasp, leaning forward for me to continue to tease her.

Seeing her like this was a thrill. I loved seeing her just obey my commands. I draped my hands over, looking at her.

"Well, it seems I found out that you were being naughty," I said to her.

"I'm sorry…Officer," she said.

I smirked. I let my hand move against there, gripping her backside, watching Tyra shudder with pleasure.

"Please, Officer, I need this," she said.

"Really now. So, you're telling me that you'll pay with your body, instead of the normal protocol? How lewd," I told her. I grabbed her butt once again, moaning.

"I don't need a ticket Officer. I can...pay in other ways to give you what you want," she said.

"Really. And how much do you want it?" I asked her. I brushed my hands there, and she moaned.

"Officer, you know I'm willing to lay it all down, and risk it all here for you," she said.

"I see. Well, if my little slut wants that, perhaps I can give you exactly what you want then. But if you don't perform well...this Officer will take you in, and the punishment will be a whole lot more," I said.

"I understand Officer," Tyra said. She looked at me, moaning in response to my touches. I simply smiled, enjoying the way that she responded to my words. I then leaned back, grabbing a pair of handcuffs from the counter.

"Follow me. A naughty girl like you deserves a proper place for punishment," I said.

I heard her moan in response, so it certainly worked out for me doing this. She followed me over to the dungeon that I crafted. This was something that I put together recently, and she'd be the first one to try it.

There were a series of bars here, and I grabbed the handcuffs, putting them between the bars. I then put her hands in there, cuffing them.

"This is good, right Officer?" she asked.

"Of course, you're doing very well so far, so easy to tease and make mine. I love seeing a beautiful woman like you become so obedient. It's quite fun to behold," I told her.

"Yes," she breathed. I moved my hands to the skirt that she wore, pulling it upward to reveal her thick ass. I touched it, watching it jiggle once more, and the delicious sounds that came out of her.

This was a thrill, and I wouldn't be convinced otherwise. I shook her butt, watching it jiggle and move slightly as she let out a small moan of surprise and pleasure.

"Well, what do you say? Do you plan to receive your punishment?" I asked her.

"Yes Officer. I've been naughty, and I'll do anything to get out of a ticket. I'd do whatever you ask of me Officer," she said.

I smiled, letting my hands graze and touch against the very tip of her backside. Then, I raised my hand, smacking her hard with it.

She let out a moan, and I shivered with delight, enjoying the way that she responded to my touch. I let my hand graze over the edge of her backside once again, touching it softly and then spanking her again. She let out another delicious moan in response to my touches, making me smile with delight.

"I see you're already giving in. You like this," I told her.

"Yes...I do," she said.

"Tell me how much you like it," I said, raising my hand once more, hearing her moan in response.

"Ahh very much!" she cried out.

"Good. I'm glad that you do. Perhaps that'll make the next part of this even more fun for you," I said.

I spanked her a couple more times watching her whimper and moan. There was a thrill that came from this

Tyra and I discussed the hard and soft limits that she had. She really didn't care as long as blood wasn't drawn. I watched her body respond to me, slowly moving as I started to let my hands move there. Then, I grabbed something else, watching her body respond to me. I started to watch her tense up, seeing what I had in my hands.

"Officer, what's that?" she said.

"Oh, this is your next punishment. You were very naughty back there, and you resisted arrest. Maybe I should add a bit more to the punishment too," I said.

I watched her tense up, seeing the delicious sounds that came out of her in response. She didn't know what would come about with this, and I was excited for it. I began to move my hands slightly, grabbing the nightstick, holding it against her ass.

I teased the flesh there, lightly pressing it and watching as she let out a small moan. She pushed her body outward and then stuck her ass out.

"Look at you, all ready to go with this," I told her.

I slowly pulled the nightstick towards her butt, lightly touching it. Then, I raised it. The smacking sound reverberated through the room, and she let out a scream. Usually, this was used for forceful reasons, but I wanted to make her feel pleasure, so I'd only keep it along the areas that felt good. That didn't mean though that I wouldn't smack her butt once or twice, touching and watching her respond to the actions that I made.

"Ahh yes," she said to me.

"What's the matter? Already so turned on you can't think straight?" I teased.

"Yes," she finally admitted.

"Well then, let's see if you can handle this then," I told her.

I grabbed the stick again, raising it by her thighs, touching them, and then smacking those areas. The area around there jiggled, and I simply smiled, enjoying the sounds that she made.

She was helpless, and I was in control. And yet, I knew for a fact that she trusted me, and wanted me to make her feel good. Feeling good was what I knew how to do best. I let my fingers drape against her backside, smacking the flesh there again, making her cry out in pleasure.

"What's the matter? You have nothing more to say?" I teased.

"I don't...this is so good. Officer, I know that I've been bad but...I love this," she said.

"Of course you do. You're a naughty little slut who likes to be teased and ordered around. There's something nice about this," I told her.

"Thank you, Officer. I'm all yours," she said to me.

"Good. As you should be," I said to her. I moved the stick right over the middle of her butt, raising it, and then hitting her hard. She howled in pleasure, and I smirked, enjoying the sounds that she made. I watched her quickly respond to every single touch of this, and there was an enjoyment that came from this. Seeing her just lose control on me like this was...quite fun to say the least, and I knew that this was a thrill that she enjoyed too.

I then hit her a few more times with this, enjoying the delicious sounds. But I wanted to see how far I could take it. How I could get her to respond to my actions and be at the mercy of my touches.

That's when I saw it.

The wand kit. This was something that I had wanted to try out. the violet wand was something that I knew some people could take, but others not so much. I knew that in the right scenarios, it would be quite a fun little experience. I soon moved my hands towards her, touching her skin on the sides. She whimpered, and I smiled.

"Now, I think you're handling your punishment very well," I told her.

"Thank you, Officer. I'll give you my body if you let me get out of this mess," she said.

I laughed.

"Of course. But it won't be right away. I want to see how much of this you can handle," I responded.

She flushed, and then, she nodded.

"Yes, give me more," she said.

I laughed, seeing her become turned on and a total mess here. There was something exciting about hearing those words.

"Good girl. And if you're satisfactory, I'm sure I can give you a little reward that you will enjoy too," I told her.

She moaned in response, and I let out a small groan of desire. I wanted to see her lose all semblance of control here, to see her just...completely dissolve into the needy slut that I knew she was.

There was something exciting about all of this, that made me ready to give everything that I wanted to towards her, and to make her squeal in response.

I prepared the wand, plugging it in and putting one of the bigger heads on there. I then moved towards her sides, seeing her whimper and shiver, and I smiled.

"Alright sweetie, this may hurt for a second. But who knows, maybe you're into that," she said.

I then put the wand gently over her, and she let out a gasp of pleasure and surprise. I started moving the wand around, hearing the sounds, the little crackling sensation of this. She let out a series of small moans, the little touches more than enough for me to enjoy. I watched her quickly respond towards me, and then, moments later, I started to run the wand against her sides, digging it in deeper, watching her cry out, the sounds lovely and delicious to me. I loved hearing her like this, and there was something about this that just turned me the fuck on.

I wanted to hear her lose control, hear her cry out in pleasure, and I knew that she was very easy to work with, to tease, and to make her lose her mind.

I started to run the wand a little further, right up against where her hipbones were, and then, I started to see her cry out, holding onto the handcuffs, the little bit of shock and surprise, along with the arousal, hitting hard.

And I loved everything about it. I continued to see her lose herself in the touches, the pleasure, and as I got right against her pubic area, I knew that she was struggling to hold back, completely immersed in the pleasure, enjoying all of the touches.

And this was something that I loved.

I enjoyed seeing her become so easy to tease.

I put the metal on there, watching her eyes widen with surprise. I wanted to see just how far I could take this before it was too much for her of course. I slowly moved the wand against her skin there, touching slightly, and she let out a small cry. There was a small redness that was there, and I couldn't help but love it. I loved seeing her become placid and easy to tease. It was a thrill, a feeling of excitement, and a desire for something else that made me just ache for her.

I moved the wand further downwards, the jolt of this making her cry out, wiggled her butt there, and made me just want to give in, to fuck her senseless. But I wanted to see her scream, to cry out, and to watch her lose all sense of herself.

I turned it up slightly, moving it there. She cried out, holding onto the bar, both moaning and staying like this.

"Officer...this is quite strong," she said.

"Of course it is. Did you think I would put this on the baby settings? You were a naughty girl, so you deserve what's coming to you," I told her.

She moaned in response to me, turned on by the words that I uttered, and I enjoyed seeing her responses. There was something exciting about seeing her just lose herself there, crying out, and enjoying the little touches and pleasure that came out of this too. I continued to run the wand there, watching her respond with the best and most delicious sounds. After a brief moment, I then stopped it, putting it off to the side, and then looking at her.

"Have you had enough?"

"No, Officer. I want more of you. I want all of you," she said.

"I see," I told her.

She looked at me, the ache, the excitement, and the obvious desire right then and there. I reached forward, grabbing her backside, touching it slightly, listening to the little moans that came out of her.

"Well, let's see what happens to you then. I want to see how you respond to me as well. Maybe you can...get away with just a pat on the butt then," I said.

I leaned forward, touching her butt, moving right behind her, and grinding against there. She let out a small cry, and I wanted nothing more than to just completely take her right then and there. I grabbed her waist, holding it there as I ground softly.

"So, tell me what you want then?" I purred into her ear.

"To...let you have me, Officer. I'm so naughty that I think I'll only learn my lesson if you give it to me," she said.

"Oh, really now? Has someone else tried to teach you a lesson before?" I asked, grabbing her butt and touching it.

"Ahh! Yes. I have been very bad. And I haven't fully learned. I may do the same bad thing again. You don't want that...right?" she said.

"Not at all. I want you to learn your lesson, once and for all of course," I told her.

She let out a small cry as I patted her butt. I thought about fucking her pussy, but I couldn't help but wonder what she would feel like if I just...took her ass tonight.

That's what I would do. But I wanted to tease her a little bit more before I did that.

And I knew the perfect way to do this.

I walked over to where I had some of the toys, getting a series of small anal beads that vibrated when turned on. I grabbed the lube, lubing it completely before slowly inserting them into her ass.

"Ahh," she said, crying out slightly.

"What's the matter"

"I wasn't...expecting this," she said.

"Well, you should always expect the unexpected. You never know what you're going to get," I told her.

I slowly slid the beads in, causing her to let out a small, garbled sound of pleasure, enjoying the little sounds that she made. Shortly afterward, I pushed it in all the way, amazed at how easy it was to tease her ass.

I knew that she was turned on, but damn this was hot. I quickly moved back, turning on the vibrations, and soon, she cried out.

As she did that, moving her body slightly, I grabbed the flogger, moving it against her legs.

"So, a naughty girl like you is already turned on by this. How cute," I said.

She let out a small moan, as I moved the flogger against her body, hitting her with the leather strings. She let out a small cry of desire, and I enjoyed seeing her like this. Seeing her just completely take it like it was nothing was a thrill that I couldn't get enough of. I started to move the flogger against her again, watching her cry out as I smacked her once more with it, watching her eyes widen with surprise.

This was a thrill. This was something that I loved, and I wanted to see her just totally lose it again and again. Every single time I moved my hands there, touching her softly, she cried out, seeing her body move forward. I reached for the vibrator, turning it up a little bit higher, seeing her respond to the actions with a little cry.

There was something just so nice about seeing her like this, seeing her just cry out with a lofty desire, a need that clearly seemed to only grow even more so. I loved hearing it, if I was going to be honest, I wanted to see her lose control.

But my cock was hard. I knew that I could continue this teasing, this tormenting, and I knew that she may want it too. But also...I ached for release, and I knew that her ass was hungry for me, hungry for the punishment that I had in mind, and I loved it.

I quickly moved myself so that I was right up against her. I started to rub her backside, watching her tense up, cry out, and enjoy this. Shortly afterward, I pulled out the beads, and each one made her utter the most delicious of sounds.

"What's the matter? Enjoying it?" I asked her.

"Yes. Very much...so," she told me.

"Well, I can give you something even more amazing to enjoy too," I said to her.

When I pulled out the beads, I put them to the side, seeing her look back at me. Her dark, beautiful skin, the eyes of pleasure that she had, this was all just so damn perfect, and I loved everything about this.

I then got myself ready, lubing myself up, spreading her cheeks, seeing her suddenly tense up, crying out as I began to slide all the way into her.

She let out a shiver, the feeling of the cock deep within her making her cry out.

"Oh, Officer. I didn't expect you to want that hole," she said.

"It was inviting, and I knew that it would be the best punishment for you," I told her.

But she seemed to enjoy it. Shortly afterward, I started to slowly move, and she let out a small cry, holding onto me there I began to press my cock deep within her, enjoying the sounds that came out of her as I did this. There was something exciting about all of this, and I had a feeling that she enjoyed this as much as I did. I then started to move myself, my cock slowly sliding in and out of her.

She let out the best sounds, making me hungry for more. I grabbed her hips, moving faster and faster, my cock fitting perfectly in her tight little ass. The heat between our bodies, the passion and desire that was there, I knew that it was only a matter of time. And she seemed to enjoy this as much as I did too.

I continued to thrust my cock into her, enjoying how tight she was, and how amazing it felt. Every single thrust, every single touch, it was all just tantalizing, and I ached for more of her. I pulled her against me, the chains rattling from the cuffs, and I moved my hands downwards. I massaged her between the legs, and she began to let out a small series of cries. She moved back, and I held onto her tightly, thrusting in deeply, enjoying the sounds that she uttered.

Every single touch, every single sound, it was all driving me completely mad, and I loved it. I soon held her close, pushing in, ramming my cock deep inside, hearing those sounds.

I knew she enjoyed this. Even though it was supposed to be a roleplay for me, I knew that she liked this too.

After a few more thrusts, I let out a small cry, holding onto her there, thrusting in as I spiled myself into her. I then felt her tense up, crying out loud as I pushed my fingers in, pumping and massaging her there, enjoying the sounds that she made. After a few more moments, she let out a small cry, enjoying it all as well.

We then finished up, both of us moving away, and after I caught my breath, I grabbed the handcuffs, getting them off her with the key that I had. She moved her hands, looking at me with a smile on her face.

"Shit that was good," she said.

"Sure was. I enjoyed every minute of it," I said.

And I meant that. It was the first time in a long time I really felt like I got this kind of enjoyment out of it. I looked at her, and she nodded.

"I wouldn't mind doing that again. I think it awoke something within me," she said.

"I hope something good," I teased.

She nodded.

"Very good honestly. And I'm glad that you could roleplay again. I knew that you wanted to stick around on the force, but they forced retirement on you," she said.

"Yeah, it sucks, but it's nice to be able to have this kind of control with someone. Anyways, I'll walk you out when you're ready?" I asked her.

She nodded.

"Of course. And you know when and where to call me when you need me for another session. I would love to explore more of this," she said to me.

I flushed, but then nodded.

"I sure would too. I figured that this is indeed something that you liked as well," I told her.

She nodded.

"Yeah, I really did," she replied.

We looked at one another, and then, I suddenly moved forward, giving her a kiss. Tyra didn't move, and instead, she accepted the kiss, letting her lips move with my own, enjoying the small, sensual touch of our lips together. Then, she pulled back, smiling.

"I wouldn't mind doing this more often if well...this is what I get out of it," she said.

"Hey, it could be. You never know," I told her.

And I meant that. It was strange to want something like that with someone, but I guess she opened up something within me.

She put on her clothes, and I paid her for the time. She was a call girl sure, but there was something else there, a deeper connection. After I paid her, I watched her go to the doorway, turning and looking me in the eyes, a smile on her face.

"Thanks," she said.

"For what?" I asked. I thought I was the one who paid her.

"For that. It really gave me…something thrilling that I loved and enjoyed. And I would do it again if you ever wanted to," she offered.

She did? I was surprised.

"I thought you just liked this for the cash," I told her, slightly taken aback by this.

"I do but…there is something exciting about the way that you treat me too. It shows me that there is that part of me, that side that likes it when I'm degraded. And I can trust you with it. I like what we have together, and I'm sure that it would be good for us," she told me.

"Yeah true," I said to her.

She then smiled, giving me one last kiss before running off. I stayed there, thinking about what had happened.

Things were interesting between Tyra and I to say the least, and I couldn't help but feel like there was something left unsaid to her. Maybe it was my imagination though, and an overreaction of course to whatever it was that she was hiding herself.

But all in all, I was just happy that I got to act out this fetish, this roleplay, and there was something thrilling about all of this. I loved it, and a part of me knew that no matter what, this would be the beginning of something more, something deeper, and something amazing for me.

I just had to hope that she would come back again, but something told me that she would, and I was more than ready to explore all of that, and everything in between that would come from this, and the fun this would begin too.

It was something that I couldn't wait for.

Her punishment

Daddy Domination, Foot Fetish

"Hey, Daddy...." I said out loud to my daddy dom, Martin.

Martin was an older man, someone who was clearly old enough to be my dad. But the two of us were in a deep and intrinsic daddy dom relationship.

He was my daddy, and I was his naughty little girl.

"I was naughty...." I said to him.

He looked at me, eying me up and down, the expression changing.

"How naughty were you?"

"I got myself off...without you around. And I broke the rule of not eating cookies before bed," I said, wiggling my butt around.

His expression changed to that of annoyance.

"Again, Princess? Didn't we have this conversation before?"

"So what? You know that it's hard to resist those cookies! And they're so good and--"

He looked at me, shaking his head.

"Addy, I thought that I told you if you disobeyed my orders once again…daddy would punish you. Is that what you want?" he asked me.

"Maybe that's what I wanted," I told him with my lip bitten. I mean, I wanted to see what he would do. He pursed his lips though, looking at me up and down.

"You are such a little shit," he said.

"Well, I just wanted a cookie. And you know how hard it is to stay sane when you want to get off, Daddy. I tried to wait but I couldn't…"

The truth was, I liked seeing him flustered when trying to deal with my shit. That was part of the fun of him being such a good daddy dom. He knew how to give out new punishments.

"Ugh, again with this…I swear, you don't make it easy for me, do you?"

"Why would I?"

"True. Well, get over here," he said.

I wondered if he was going to spank me, but then, he pushed me down onto the bed, grabbing my chin and looking at me up in my eyes.

"You're going to get the punishment of your life, and one that'll show you why you shouldn't disobey Daddy," he said to me, his voice dark as he said that.

I didn't know why, but I felt excited about that.

However, what I didn't know was the way his hands moved downward, getting right over the top of my feet, touching right then and there.

"Hey wait a minute—"

"No, Princess. This is your punishment. Daddy isn't happy that you disobeyed him. And this isn't the first time you did it either," he purred.

He wasn't wrong. I mean...sometimes I was a bit of a brat and liked to test my limits with how far I could go and take punishment. But not like this.

"Please, Daddy, I promise I'll be good and—"

"No, this time...you'll be getting quite the punishment. And maybe if you're a good girl and beg enough, you'll get daddy's cock," he said.

The sound of that was enough to make me moan to be honest. I wanted him, and I knew that me teasing him like this was quite fun. There was something thrilling about this, about the way that he already had the punishment laid out.

But my feet were a source of great irritation and pleasure to me. the truth was...daddy had a foot fetish. And sometimes he would use that as a punishment for me. Much to both my dismay and of course my enjoyment.

He would tease my feet, making me shiver and moan with delight, enjoying the way that I sounded, and he would continue to tease me, watching me respond to him, seeing both the pleasure and the distaste that came from this was always an enjoyable thing.

"Alright, you decided to disobey me. Now...I'm going to make sure you learn your lesson, Princess," he said.

"Oh, I bet you will," I said.

He then pulled off the bottom part of my stockings, leaving my feet bare. Shit, this is going to be even worse. I started to feel his hands move downward after pulling the stockings off, moving to the base of my feet and touching them. He examined my feet, making me gasp and shiver as I felt the touch there. His hands were a little bit colder, but I couldn't help but enjoy the way that this felt.

"Now, Princess, you're over here disobeying Daddy. You seem to like it when I punish you," he said.

His hands moved towards the middle of my feet. It wasn't even a massage or anything, but it made me gasp.

"Ahh," I said.

"Well? What do you have to say for yourself?" he said.

"Daddy.... the feeling...."

It was both incredibly pleasurable, but also sensitive. And yet, I loved everything about this. Daddy began to move his hands there, just barely touching the soles of my feet. But the little touch alone was enough to drive me fucking mad, making me shiver, cry out with delight, enjoying the pleasure that came off of this. It was so sensitive that I had no clue what else to do, other than of course to just let out a small cry, touching the tip of the bed, and feeling his hand slowly move there.

"I'm going to take care of your feet Princess since I know how much you love it when I do that," he purred into my ear.

Every little touch made me shiver, the very edge of his hand touching the tip of my foot, making me shiver and cry out.

"There you go. You trying to hold back those cute little moans of yours? How adorable," he said in my ear.

I was struggling to hold back. I wanted to moan and scream out loud, but I was trying not to show the pleasure that this was giving me.

I hated that my feet were so sensitive, that it turned me into a pile of goo like this. But as Martin did this, letting his fingers touch there, I started to move around.

"Hold still, or else I'll put the restraints on your feet," he said.

"Ahh, Daddy," I said to him. I liked the idea of being restrained, and at the mercy of his foot touches.

There was something so damn hot about that. His hands then moved towards the very tips of my feet, moving towards the toes, and that little area behind them that was very sensitive. He rubbed his hands there, and as he let his fingers graze against the very tip of the back of my foot, I cried out, holding the sheets and moaning in response. He smiled, watching me slowly come undone, and the control that came out of this.

"So, Princess, do you think you can handle this?" he asked me.

I wanted to prove that I could handle this. That's all I wanted, and I knew for a fact that he enjoyed seeing me slowly come undone like this. He let his hands roam and tickle against there, and as he did this, I let out a small cry, enjoying the touch of his hands, feeling it all just completely overtake me to the point where even I wasn't sure what to make of this anymore.

He then ran his fingers against the underside, pressing there, and when he did that, I let out a jolt, crying out loud in pleasure, and moaning in response to this. I reacted immediately, enjoying the touch. The sensitive nature of his hand against my foot, and what it created within me was something I both loved and hated.

It was strange to be at the mercy of this man, to enjoy every possible moment, every type of touch that came out of this, and I knew that he was enjoying the little tormented groans and moans that I made. He let his hands touch there, teasing against the edge of my foot, and as he did that, I let out a moan, tensing up, brushing my hips upward until finally, I let out a small cry, coming down from the high that I experienced, and then, moments later he pulled back, seeing that look there in my eyes.

"Well, Princess, looks like you enjoyed your little punishment," he said.

"No, I didn't, Daddy. You know how sensitive my feet are," I said with a pout. Of course, there was also something arousing about it.

I hated to admit that the feeling of my feet was such a turn-on, but then he smiled.

"Well, perhaps I can make this even harder on you too. In fact, Daddy does like how cute your feet are. I noticed your toenails were nicely painted recently. Did you do that for Daddy?" he asked.

I looked at him, flushing.

"Yes, Daddy., I figured that you would like it," I told him.

"Well, I sure do. I love the color," he said.

Hearing him praise me was like a drug to me. I let out a small gasp.

"Do you want to see more of me, Daddy? I also got myself ready for you, even though I know you have to punish me," I said.

"Well, we can see where we're at, and I'll see what kind of punishment I want to give to you," he said.

I moaned in response, turned on by the punishment that he had planned. Even though I had no clue what it was, a part of me figured it would be something pretty big, and something that he enjoyed too.

"What's the punishment then, Daddy?" I finally asked with a blush.

He pursed his lips, and then he spoke.

"Get on your hands and knees, Princess," he said.

My hands and knees? What did he plan to do with that? I wanted to ask him, but then I quickly got on all fours, my butt sticking out. He reached out, touching my backside and massaging it.

"Your butt is getting nice and big," he said to me.

"Thank you, Daddy," I said.

Then, he grabbed the panties I wore, taking them off. He still left the skirt on, but I felt exposed as his hand reached forward, touching the very tip of my butt. He let his hands move there, and I let out a small gasp of surprise, enjoying every single moment of his touch. He let his fingers graze against there, and even just the tiniest of touches was setting me off.

"Daddy, please," I said.

"Please, what, Princess? I have no clue what it is that you want," he said.

He was definitely feigning innocence here. I wiggled my butt around, and then, he started to smile.

"Well, my naughty girl definitely has been bad, but maybe I should make the punishment something a little bit...different," he said.

"How different, Daddy?" I asked him.

I heard the sound of a drawer open, and then, I felt a vibrator up against my ass. I shivered, moaning out loud as he started to slowly move it in.

I wasn't used to anal, but it was obvious that was the point of this punishment. He wanted to see me squirm, and what better way than well…this. I felt the toy begin to slowly shimmy its way into me, and then, I let out a small gasp of surprise, enjoying the feeling of this. I started to move my hips forward, enjoying the touch of this, but then he pushed it all the way in, turning it on.

The feeling of this sent shivers through my entire body, and it turned me on more than I cared to admit. I started to feel him push it up to the highest settings, making me gasp out with pleasure, but I also knew it would take a whole lot more than this to get me off.

"That's part of your punishment. Mostly because I know how much you utterly enjoy the feeling of your ass being filled," he said.

"I don't, Daddy. Please let me take this out," I asked him.

"No no. You're getting your punishment for being a very naughty girl. Now first, this," he said.

He moved his lips downward, and I expected him to eat me out until of course, I was close, and then he would stop. But he didn't do that.

No, he did something so much worse. He moved his lips downward until of course, he was right near the entrance of my pussy. I felt his tongue start to slowly snake out, licking there for a moment, but then trail down my legs. I whimpered in shock and surprise until he got to my feet.

He took the top part of my foot, touching it there. He then massaged the tip of it, making me whimper and moan with pleasure.

"There we go. Such a good girl," he said.

"Thank you...Daddy," I told him, unable to properly think straight because of this.

"But what if Daddy did this?"

What did he plan to—

Oh, this was it. A tongue snaked out, moving against the front part of my foot, and I let out a small moan, pushing myself forward, completely lost in the feeling of this. He teased the very tip of my foot, and the touch of it alone was enough to drive me completely insane. He then chuckled, letting his tongue move outwards until of course, he had it around my toes, licking and sucking on my feet there.

I knew daddy had a foot fetish, but I also feel like he was doing this on purpose because he wanted to see me squirm. And squirming was something that I very much did as soon as I felt the hands there, and tongue skirt on downwards.

Fuck I was already such a turned-on mess, and it didn't help that he got a kick out of this too.

He then moved his tongue away, the sliminess of my feet making me moan, but only then did I feel the feather there, draped against my toes.

I also felt something else there. I didn't know what it was until of course, he turned it on, and I felt the massager against my feet.

I let out a small cry, moaning and crying out in response to the actions at hand. Why did this feel so damn good? What was he trying to accomplish here? I don't even know, but I let out a low, guttural sound, holding onto the bed as he massaged my feet with the massager.

"Holy shit," I told him.

"What's the matter, Princess?"

"This is just…it's so damn strong. I don't know what else to tell you," I finally spat out.

I felt like I was experiencing a whole different world as I uttered the words. A world that I didn't even know much about, and yet, there was a thrill that came out of this, a thrill that I liked so much more than I cared to admit, and I knew that he liked it too.

He then moved the massager up my leg, moving towards my inner thigh, barely grazing the edge of this. I cried out, holding onto there, feeling the excitement and desire of my body making me enjoy it all right then and there.

I started to watch his hands move downward until of course, they got to my legs. I was already a panting, sweating mess.

"Alright, Princess, it looks like you did well with this part of your punishment. Perhaps Daddy would like to see your cute body now," he told me.

Of course he did. I started to move my body so that I sat there, looking at him.

"Take off your clothes, Princess. Daddy wants to see all of you," he said.

I flushed, feeling like his eyes were right on my own as I started to move my hands upward, undoing the top part of the lingerie that I wore. It was a string, and when I did that, it tumbled down, moving it out of my way. I did the back strap too, revealing my breasts, which were aching for his touch.

He looked at me, smiling as I sat there, flush crimson against him.

"That's not all I want to see removed sweetie," he said.

Fuck did he mean...my bottom half too? Probably, because he wanted to see me naked there. He simply watched me as I took off the skirt, pulling it off. I then took my panties off, revealing my naked body, which he simply admired.

"You look wonderful, Princess. Now don't forget, your punishment is to have that toy inside of you while Daddy teases you. And you aren't to orgasm until you beg for it, or I tell you to," he said to me.

I flushed, feeling a bit exposed by this, and this alone. Did he get a thrill from doing this? Probably, but I knew that there wasn't any way for me to stop this, and yet, in a strange way, I didn't want this to stop.

"Okay, Daddy. Please...take me. Explore me and make me feel good. I promise I won't cum until you say so," I said to him.

"Very good girl. I'll take great care of you," he said.

He let his fingers drape down until of course, he got to where my breasts were, touching the very tip of them slightly, watching me suddenly shiver and cry out with pleasure at the sensation of this. He simply moved his hands against my nipple, pressing against there, moving his hands slightly. The little touch against the nub was enough to drive me crazy, and then, moments later, I started to feel his fingers there, pinching against the very edge of my nipple, rolling it. As he did that, I let out a small cry, enjoying the feeling of this, the touch that came with it, and the excitement that this brought me.

"Daddy," I cried out, feeling like I was about to burst already. He simply chuckled, touching me slightly there, watching my eyes widen with surprise as he did this.

"Well, Princess, what do you think. Do you want something more?" he asked me.

"Yes," I cried out.

"Good...maybe I'll let you cum then," he said.

He moved his hands against my nipple, teasing and pinching it. I felt like I was about to burst right then and there, go crazy as he did this. But maybe I could hold back. I sure as shit hoped that I could.

He continued to dance his fingers on my nipple, making me bite my tongue and moan out loud. Moments later, he moved his hands downward, touching the very tip of my pussy, letting his hand move there. I cried out, feeling like I was a mess, and completely at the mercy of this man's touches and feelings. He continued this, holding me there as he looked into my eyes.

"Well, Princess? You're going to have to ask Daddy for it," he said.

He wanted me to beg. I knew that daddy liked seeing me in this state. I flushed, biting my lip and then speaking.

"Please…Daddy," I told him.

"Please what? I can't possibly help you if I don't know what you want," he said.

The rat bastard was trying to get me to lose control. I held my breath, and then, tried to withstand the ache, the pleasure, and the need.

"Please give it to me," I told him.

He looked me in the eyes, and then he smiled.

"Well, you'll need to do a little bit better than that."

"Please, Daddy! Fuck my pussy," I said, completely at a loss on how to hold back, and what to say. He looked me in the eyes, and then, moments later he smiled.

"Well, since you asked so nicely and with such a cute and needy sound, I guess I can give it to you," he said to me.

He was doing this to be a tease, and then, moments later, he moved toward my pussy, moving his fingers against the very tip of my clit. He rubbed there, little touches and strokes, and I cried out, completely enraptured by daddy's touches. I knew that he enjoyed the sounds, and I was completely lost in the feeling of this. Moments later, he pushed his fingers harder against my clit there, touching me harder. I let out a choked sound as he continued to explore me, pushing his fingers in. I was completely enamored in the feeling, enjoying his touches, the way his hands moved about, and the sensations there. He then began to pump within me, and he was just barely missing that one spot, causing me to tense up, cry out loud, and feel like I needed to beg for it.

"Please," I said.

"Please what, Princess? I can barely hear what you are saying," he said.

The bastard was trying to get me to slowly lose control. But I sighed, feeling completely amazed by how turned on and horny I was.

"Please...fuck me," I told him.

He looked at me, smiling.

"Well, if you put it that way, I'm sure that I can give you that. But first, I want you to have a taste of me, of Daddy's cock," he said.

I felt like salivating as he said those words. I wanted him so badly, and the ache was driving me crazy. I struggled with thinking straight, with everything that was going on, and for a long time, I simply just laid there, holding onto the restraints and looking at him. He then undid his pants, pulling them downwards, and that's when I saw his member, standing fully at attention, making me shiver and crave more.

It was a hunger that I couldn't merely explain, but then, when he pushed it into my mouth, letting me move my tongue against the tip, I was about to go completely mad. I slowly took him further and further into my mouth, feeling the rush of pleasure, and the excitement of this. I soon felt his cock move further down my throat, making me shiver and tense up, enjoying every single moment of this. I licked the underside, savoring the taste of his long cock, before he started to lightly touch the very tip of me, thrusting in and out, enjoying the touch of this, and I knew that he was enjoying this as much as I was. I continued to touch, to tease him, and as we did this, I knew that he liked this too. He continued to move his hips there, but then, moments later, he pulled back.

I gave him a look of mild annoyance. I thought he'd continue this, but I guess not. He soon looked at me, smiling.

"Alright there, Princess, I think you've had enough. And honestly, Daddy is at his limit too," he said.

I flushed, but then nodded, feeling his cock move slowly against me, teasing my folds. I bit my lip, letting out a small, breathy sound as he slowly pushed himself all the way in, and then, as he did that, he looked me in the eyes, the thrill of it all hitting us. He slowly moved his cock deep within me, and as he did that, I sat there, completely held in place by how good this was, and how just...amazing he was. Every single thrust, every single touch, it was all enough to drive me slowly but surely to the point of madness. I gripped the area, and as he continued to plunge himself into me, holding me there, I wanted more.

I wanted him to take my breath away.

I loved being choked. His hands were perfect against me, touching me like that, and as I was getting close, my body completely languid, I started to cry out.

"Daddy," I said to him.

"What is it, Princess?" he asked.

"Choke...me," I told him.

He gave me that catlike smile, holding his hands to my throat, cupping where he always made me feel good. It was then when, moments later, he started to thrust deep into me, holding me there. I let out a series of small sounds, and that's when I felt it.

The sudden, amazing force of my orgasm. It hit every fiber of my being, making me suddenly tense up, holding onto me, crying out as I felt the throes of this overtake me. Moments later, he continued his relentless thrusts, my body starting to feel the exhaustion. It was then when, after a few more thrusts, he pulled his hand away, plunging into me.

But as he did so, filling me with his seed, he gave me a long, passionate kiss. We stayed like this, kissing hard as he released. When he was finally done, he pulled back, seeing my body stay there, completely languid as I tried to figure out what to say to him. I wasn't going to lie, I felt good, but also...I wanted to know how he felt too.

When the high of the orgasm finally came down, we looked at one another. He undid the restraints, holding them there, and when I looked at him, I smiled.

"That was amazing, Daddy," I told him.

"You're good, Princess? Let me make sure your arms are okay," he said.

As he did so, he grabbed some lotion cream and rubbed it in the bruises that formed there. It wasn't the first time I accidentally had some injuries afterward, but he always took care of me. After he finished, he looked at me, seeing the spent nature of my body.

"So how do you feel?"

"Good. Tired as shit. That was...something all right," I told him. I didn't expect things to go like that. He looked at me, and then, he nodded.

"Yeah, you held out like a trooper there. I'm quite proud of you," he said.

"Thank you, Daddy," I told him.

He leaned in, giving me a long, passionate kiss as he pulled away.

"Well, you want to go over and take a shower? And don't worry, we don't have to have the dynamic," he told me.

I looked at him, feeling a bit of a flush ghost my face. I then took a deep breath, holding onto the bed there for a moment, smiling contentedly.

"Yeah, I'd like that," I told him.

He helped me up since I was fucked too silly to move, and I knew for a fact that I was completely spent, but also happy too. I was glad to have someone as amazing as this man, as cool as he was, and as we went over there, I struggled to move, but he helped me every step of the way.

And I couldn't thank him enough. I loved that about him. I loved that he was my daddy, and he would take care of me no matter what. I just wanted to spend the rest of my life with him, and I wanted him to take care of me, through thick and thin.

We took a shower together, both of us kissing one another. After we got out of the bedroom, we stopped the dynamic as much, and instead were two different people. I felt good though, and as he finished with this, he looked at me.

"So…you want to try that again?" he asked me.

I beamed, nodding.

"Yeah, I'd love to," I told him.

It was something I desired far more than I cared to admit. He looked at me, beaming.

"Well, I'm sure the two of us can plan something like that again. And I'm sure you did enjoy the punishment that you got too," he teased.

That's right. The feet. I flushed as I thought about it. I mean, I didn't find it to be the worst punishment he's given, that's for sure, and in a sense, I wouldn't mind that being a punishment again.

"Yeah, I wouldn't mind a punishment like that," I told him.

"Well, perhaps next time I'll go a little easier and give you a punishment that you can enjoy," he said.

I immediately felt excited just hearing those words. There was something super fun about this, and I knew that he liked this too. After a little bit, I nodded.

"Well, there is always next time, and I can't wait for the fun that we can share together...Daddy," I said.

He touched my head as it was under the shower, his wet hand meeting my wet hair.

"Of course, Princess. I'll always take care of you, no matter what," he said.

And when he uttered those words, I believed him. I truly, utterly did. There was something super honest about it, and I knew for a fact that he meant it when he said those words. I felt good, and I knew that he liked this too. For a long time, we stayed like this, enjoying one another, and I knew for a fact that this was the beginning of something more.

I was completely happy and smitten about this, and I knew that things were going to get better. He was so good to me, and I knew that I could always rely on daddy, no matter what it may be. There was something about this that made me excited, and I was more than ready for more, and ready to see just what may come about from here on out, and the fun that would begin.

He definitely had something else planned for me in the future, and I knew that he had a lot going on as well. But I also knew that he'd take care of me and that he'd be there for me, no matter what.

And that of course was something that I could rely on, that I could trust, and that I could accept no matter what.

The Forbidden Girl

Forbidden Romance, Bisexual Threesome

There she was.

Standing at the edge of the smoking area near the lab. It was Millie, and she was there with her boyfriend Jude. Two of the smartest people here in the area and two people who I thought were incredibly attractive.

And there I was, just a lowly intern.

Millie turned to me, taking one last drag and then looking over at me.

"Hey there Cammy. What's up?" she asked.

"Oh, nothing. Just taking a break. You two seem to be doing well, making names for yourselves aren't you?" I asked her.

"Yeah, we managed to submit our thesis over to the examiner, and they loved it. We'll be publishing that in the science journal next month," she said.

"Wow, I wish I was half as smart as you two," I told them.

Jude laughed.

"Well, you're working under us. I'm sure our tutelage and other characteristics will rub off on you. You're a bright and beautiful young woman Cammy," he said, giving me a wink.

I blushed, realizing that he called me such nice things. It made my heart skip a beat, the excitement of this driving me wild.

"Thank you," I told him.

"You're welcome," he said with a wink.

Millie and Jude went back inside, leaving me out here alone. I couldn't shake the feeling that I had, the desire for both of them. But I sure as shit knew it wouldn't become anything.

For starters, both Millie and Jude were together. They couldn't possibly want someone like me. I didn't think Millie was bisexual either. She never gave off the vibe, at least that's what I got from it. I also knew that Jude was kind of a flirt.

And not just that, they're two of the top researchers, meanwhile I'm just a lowly intern, begging to be found and seen as someone different from the rest of them.

There was no way the two of them would even take notice of me, even ironically. Which sucked, but oh fucking well.

I flushed thinking about this, unsure of what to say or even what to do at this point. There was clearly a whole lot that I wanted to just spit out and tell them, but I didn't dare bother them with it. It would make shit even worse you know.

Which was why I kept to myself, and I kept all of these feelings deep within me. that's the best way to do this, and the only way to have some sort of solace.

Over the next couple of months though, I started working more and more with Millie and Jude. Both of them included me like I was a part of their team without officially mentioning it. There was something thrilling about that, and something that I liked. But would it lead to anything more? Or was it just my imagination getting the best of me.

However, one day I was approached by Jude, who kept looking away as he tried to avoid eye contact with me.

"Something the matter there Jude?" I inquired.

"Oh, it's nothing," he said.

"You say that, but I see the nervousness in your eyes," I told him.

"Well, it's just...we wanted you to come work with us for this next experiment. We want you included on the research paper with us," he said.

Was he serious about this? I flushed, seeing the way his eyes looked down on me.

He meant it.

"Are you sure about that? I don't want to be a bother or anything," I said.

"You kidding me? you're far from a bother hun," he told me with a smile.

I appreciated hearing that because I felt like I was in the shadow of them. And his eyes were soft.

"Sure, I can help then," I told him.

He beamed, taking my hand and holding it.

"Then let's get started," he replied.

He brought me over to the room where Millie and he worked. They had their own private lab. I worked in here sometimes, but mostly just used this to report to them. But upon looking at this even more, I started to realize just how...nice this place was.

Their lab was easily one of the best, and I was a bit jealous that they had such a nice setup.

"Wow, this is cool," I told him.

"Thanks. Anyways, I'll have Millie brief you on what we're studying and what you can help with," he said.

His hand lingered for a split second on my shoulder before leaving. I felt a bit nervous, especially since I was alone with them.

Two of the hottest people that I knew and both of them were way the fuck out of my league. I was a little embarrassed to admit it, but I knew the way I felt was the truth.

Shortly after, Millie showed up, looking me up and down and beaming.

"There you are," she said.

"Hey, sorry about that," I told her.

"Oh, you're good. You should know by now that we usually don't start this shit till way later. Anyways, I guess I can brief you on what we're trying to accomplish here," she told me.

"Yeah, that would be nice," I told her.

"Well, here's the outline. If you have questions, ask me," she said.

I read it over, and then, moments later, we started to work.

But I noticed there was something left unsaid. It was clear that Millie and Jude both wanted to say something, whatever it may be. I flushed thinking about this, knowing that both of them had something on the back of their mind. I wanted to ask, but I was afraid that it may come off as a bit rude.

But I did wonder this. I was curious about how they well…felt about me. I noticed Millie's eyes gazing over my body and a small smile on her face.

"Something the matter?" I finally asked her.

"Oh, it's nothing. I'll ask you later," she told me.

I wondered what Millie wanted to say to me. I also noticed that Jude's eyes kept lingering against my body too.

Were they both hiding something that they wanted to say? Or was this just them acting a bit weird and all. I wanted to know, but I was afraid I'd be bothering them far too much.

We worked on the experiments well into the night, when I saw Millie take a deep breath, looking over at me.

"What's...the matter?" I asked her.

"Oh, it's nothing. Sorry, I'm a bit distracted by thoughts," she said to me.

What thoughts were distracting her so badly? But I wanted to ask. I felt a little nervous that I was prying into affairs that technically weren't a goddamn part of my business. But as we continued to work together, I felt the tension grow.

Maybe she was holding back certain feelings. But then, as we finished with the last of the experiments, she turned to me, smiling.

"We're done for the day. Thanks for everything, Cammy," she said.

"No, thank you, Millie. It's a thrill to work underneath you," I told her.

It seemed like it was a good thing, but maybe I was overthinking all of this. Millie looked away, taking a moment to process whatever was going through her head.

"Something the matter?"

"No, it's just...there was something I wanted to tell you, but I fear that it may be a little too embarrassing. I don't want to make you uncomfortable or anything," she said.

"You can tell me. I want to hear it," she said.

She then turned to me, looking me in the eyes, and then, she cupped my chin, pulling it so that she looked at me directly in the eyes. I looked at her, lust and desire obvious there, but there was also something else there. A little bit of concern.

"What is...this?" I asked her.

"Something I wanted to ask you for a while, Cammy. I think actions speak a little bit louder than words here though," she told me.

"What do you mean by actions and—"

As I said those words, she continued to kiss me. I suddenly felt completely immersed in the feeling of her lips against mine, and while this wasn't what I expected, I quickly and eagerly enjoyed it, kissing her passionately and deeply. She and I stayed like this for a long while, until finally, she moved back, smiling.

"I knew it," she purred.

"What do you mean?" I asked, unsure if that was a good thing or not.

"I knew you had a little crush on me. You kind of suck at hiding these things," she said.

"I...I do?" I asked her.

"Yeah, you do. And it's okay because I'm sure that Jude wouldn't mind either. He's been waiting for me to find a cute little friend to tease and have fun with, and I think you may be the one," she said.

She wanted me as a plaything? I thought she just thought I was attractive, not like this!

"Are you serious?" I asked her.

"Does it look like I'm fucking around here?" she said with a chuckle.

"No...."

"Well good. I'm glad that you see things my way. So, my dear, what do you think. Want to have a little bit of fun?" she asked.

Did she really want to fuck me this much? It surprised me to say the least, but I quickly nodded.

"I appreciate this, and I kind of...do want it. But what about Jude?" I asked her.

I didn't want to overstep any boundaries that she had with him. but then, she laughed.

"You kidding me? he's the one who put me up to this. Right honey?" she asked.

"Indeed," Jude said, his hands on my waist, his eyes looking into my own, grinding against me. I let out a small gasp, surprised by this.

Both of these people wanted me, these attractive as shit people who already had me as putty in their hands.

And yet, I couldn't stop thinking about this, and how good this was. I quickly nodded.

"Sure, but where?" I asked.

"Where do you think? Follow me," Jude said.

I did as he said, making our way over to the small little guest room attached to the lab. This was supposed to be a room that was used when you had to stay late. But I guess this worked here. Before I knew it, I was on the bed, and then, Millie's lips were on my own.

They were so soft and subtle, and I couldn't get enough of this. I quickly kissed her back. It was the first time I'd kissed a woman before, and honestly...I liked this. Meanwhile, Jude's hands moved against the sides of my body, touching me there. He skirted his hands upwards, until of course he got to my breasts, touching them slightly, making me shiver and cry out, turned on by this whole thing.

"Fuck," I said out loud.

"You good? Or are you just aroused by the mere touch?" he said.

"I'm...aroused," I told him.

"As you should be. You have a cute body there Cammy. Millie told me that she had a crush on you for a while, and I figured...why not have fun. We've always wanted to try a third, and see how it goes," he said.

"Indeed," Millie said, pulling away, smiling as she touched my chin. I started to flush, enjoying the touch of her hands.

"That would be nice," I told her.

"Good. Then that settles it," she said.

She moved her hands so that they were right up against the tips of my nipples from outside the shirt. I suddenly let out a small gasp, moaning in response as I put my hips upwards, enjoying the idea of both of these attractive people taking me like this.

It was like a dream come true, if I do say so myself.

And I honestly wanted this. Millie's hands moved towards my sides, while Jude's then moved upward, touching me from outside my bra. The little touch was more than enough, and I quickly let out a small gasp, enjoying the feeling of his hands. He started to move his hands under my bra, playing with my nipples as he turned his head towards mine, kissing me.

Jude was a good kisser too. No wonder both of these people were so good for one another. I was a bit jealous I couldn't have this for myself, but this was clearly the next best thing.

Then, Millie moved towards me, our lips and tongues moving and teasing one another. Jude did the same, our lips and tongues all fitting together in an interesting way. I couldn't get enough of it though, and I enjoyed everything that both of these attractive people brought to the table.

I ached for more, I craved their touch, and then, before I knew it, I felt his lips move back, and he bit down on my neck, licking and teasing there.

Then, it was just Millie and me. Her lips felt so perfect, and that, combined with the touch was something that I enjoyed a whole lot too. I soon noticed her lips move forward, the tongue massaging my own, and I ached for her.

"Fuck," I said.

"You like this?" she teased.

"Yes," I breathed.

"Then maybe we can have a little more fun then," Jude said, moving his hands downwards, grabbing the hem of my shirt.

I mean, I was already pretty far gone, and I wanted to feel more of this too. I started to nod.

"Please," I said, aching for more, craving the touch of their hands, and the pleasure.

Jude quickly did away with my shirt, and then moved toward my bra. He undid it, leaving me topless in the room with both of them. I saw Millie's eyes widen, and a catlike smile form on her face.

"You have such cute breasts," she said.

"Thank...you," I said.

I expected her to just touch them, but she soon captured one of the nipples against her mouth, sucking on the flesh there. I let out a cry, feeling her suck on the flesh. She moved her tongue against the edge, and I laid there, feeling the blissful sensation of this. She then let her tongue move around, teasing the area slightly, while her other hand pinched the nipple, causing me to let out a small moan of surprise, enjoying everything about this. It was like I was experiencing a whole different world, and I loved everything about it.

I craved more of her touch, desired the feeling completely, and then, I felt her hand pinch my other nipple, causing me to tense up.

Jude simply smiled, watching Millie's hands get grabby, touching every part of me.

"This is fun isn't it?" he said to Millie.

"Yes dear," she said.

She pulled back, looking at me, and then I moved down, grabbing at her shirt. I didn't want to be the only one like this. Millie then smiled.

"Of course you get a taste too," she said.

She pulled off the lab coat, and then undid her shirt. She then pulled off her bra, revealing her large, perky tits.

I reached out, touching them and watching her let out a small moan in response to the touches that I brought to her.

"She likes that," I heard Jude say.

"I'm sure," I said.

My hands got grabby, exploring every part of her. This was...different to say the least. I liked the idea of this, and Millie seemed to like it too.

Her breasts were so much bigger than mine that touching them felt so damn different. But she didn't seem to mind it either, and I liked feeling her up, and the sounds that she made. They were delicious, but also something that I could definitely get used to as well.

"Wow, you like them too," she said.

I put my lips against her nipple, pressing there, enjoying the sounds that came out of her. I started to pinch the other nipple, loving everything from this, and I saw for a moment the pleasure that was obvious on her face.

Jude seemed to like this too, but I could also tell that he wanted a little bit of the action as well.

I then moved back, laying down, hiking up my skirt to show my black panties. I rubbed them slightly, looking at Millie.

"If you want a taste..."

She grinned, spreading me apart, letting her lips move up the sides of my thighs, smiling at me.

"But of course. And you can give Jude a little bit of attention too," she said.

I nodded.

"Yes," I breathed out.

Her hands were right there against my panties, grabbing the waistband and holding it there. She looked me in the eyes, beaming, and then she slowly pulled them down. I looked at her, surprised by this, and she soon spread me apart, letting her fingers move against there.

"You're so cute, and I can see how sensitive you are already," she said.

Her little touches were more than enough for me, but then, I felt my own hands move upward, undoing the zipper and fly on Jude's pants, pulling them down to reveal his large, aching member. I looked at him, quickly pulling his cock closer to me.

It was big, much bigger than I expected. But there was something about this that turned me the hell on. I wanted this, and I knew that he did too. I let my tongue move out, teasing the very tip of his cock, hearing the sounds of approval directly from him. As I licked there, I slowly moved my lips against there, sucking and teasing the very edges of this, watching him cry out loud and then, I pushed about halfway down, sucking him off.

Meanwhile, I felt Millie's hands against me, slowly lick every part of me. She teased my clit, causing me to let out a small gasp of surprise, thrusting forward, enjoying the different feelings from this. He began to push it deeper down my throat, and she moved her tongue there, teasing the tip of my clit, sucking on it too. I let out a cry, muted by the cock that was there, but I didn't care, I liked it.

I loved feeling like I was their bitch. I noticed Millie spread me apart further, sliding a finger inside, and I let out a small gasp that was muffled once again. I pushed my lips further downward, and then, shortly afterward, I felt it hit the base of my throat. I gasped, enjoying the feeling of gagging, and he began to hold my head, fucking my mouth while his wife continued to eat me out, thrusting her fingers in and out of me. She pushed two fingers in, dipping deep inside, and then she pushed in harder, causing me to let out a small gasp, a needy sigh, and felt like I was losing every part of me.

I ached for more, the feeling of Jude inside of me, and for well...just a taste of Millie.

I was close already, and I felt the fingers press upward, teasing that one spot of mine. As she pushed there, I let out a small, garbled sound, enjoying it, and then, moments later, he pulled back, looking at me.

"You have such a good mouth, but I need to be inside of you," he said.

"You...you do?" I said.

"Yes," he said.

I felt Millie's tongue tease and continue, and while I loved the feeling, I knew that I needed to taste her too. Moments later, she pulled back, smiling.

"What was that honey?" she said.

"I need to be inside one of you now," he said.

"Well, why not me first, and then you can finish in her. Give her something to remember us by. You're on the pill, right?" Millie said, turning to me with the last line.

I flushed, but then nodded.

"Y-yeah, I am," I said.

"There we go, problem solved," Millie said.

But I already felt like I was at my limit. I ached for more, and I knew that she wanted to give me more.

She then moved herself towards Jude, pushing him down on the bed. She then slid over him, pushing herself all the way down, looking at me with a look of lust, pure desire, and need.

"Fuck this is good," she said.

I looked at her, riding his cock, and I craved a touch. I wanted to feel her. I quickly scurried over, moving my lips towards the very edge of her pussy, licking the tip of her clit.

"Holy shit," Millie said, moving herself up and down. I began to tease the very tip of her clit, enjoying the sounds that came out of her as she continued to move herself up and down, enjoying the sensation of my lips and tongue. I began to move my lips a bit harder, sucking on her clit as she continued to ride.

Millie moved her body, and I reached up, pinching her nipples as I took a moment to feast on her. The sounds that she made, the movements of her body, all of this was driving me crazy, turning me the fuck on, and I loved every passing moment of this. I craved for more of this, and I needed to feel more of this too.

I continued to move my lips around, letting my tongue tease her. She let out a series of small gasps and moans, and I knew that she was close. But then, moments later she moved her hands to my shoulder, riding Jude until she let out a small cry.

I expected her to finish with a moan, but then she grabbed my face, pulling me closer, letting her lips move there. I quickly moved my own lips to hers as she pulled away, gasping as she was finished.

"Fuck that was good," she said.

"I can tell," I replied.

"Get on," she told me, motioning to Jude's cock. He was big, and Millie just took him like it was nothing. I was a tad bit jealous, but I didn't want to disappoint. I moved my body so that it was right over his cock, sliding down on it, looking at him with a smile as I felt him all the way in.

Fuck he was big. It took me a moment to get used to this, but then I moved a little bit. However, he grabbed my hips, pushing me so that I was on my knees. He then moved all the way in, causing me to let out a small cry of surprise and need as he plunged himself.

"Holy...shit," I said out loud. I was surprised by this. It was a different sensation, and it was one that I definitely enjoyed. I started to feel him thrust deep into me, making me tense up and moan in response. Everything about this just felt so damn good, and I craved the feeling of this, the touch that drove me insane, and the ache for so much more.

He started to thrust himself deep in there, plunging into me, making me cry out loud, aching for him as I started to feel as if I was about to lose it right then and there. I was definitely ready, and I knew that no matter what, everything was going to be amazing. He filled me up, holding onto my hips as he plunged in deep, but then, I saw Millie there, her pussy right there in my face, and I soon took a moment to explore her, touching the tip with my tongue, and then moving my tongue inside, exploring and enjoying her folds.

She let out a small gasp, holding me there as I continued to tease her with my tongue, feeling her gasp and moan in response to everything that I did. This was heavenly to me, especially since it just...felt so right to me. it felt like it was what she wanted, and I knew that she was close again.

"Fuck Cammy you're amazing," she said, holding my head there. I pushed my tongue in, letting it sink into her, teasing that one spot, and as soon as I hit there, she tensed up, crying out loud, and then, she held onto me as she finished up.

Moments later, I felt something else push deep into me, holding me there as I let out a low, guttural sound. I felt a hand move to my clit, rubbing there as I felt the throes of pleasure hit me. it was then when I cried out, letting out a sound, and the feeling of release hit me.

As I felt this, his own cock pushed all the way in, filling me up with his seed fully and completely, enjoying the touch of this.

He then moved back, looking me in the eyes with a smile, enjoying the feeling of this.

"You good?" he asked me.

He pulled out, and I simply laid there, enjoying the feeling that this gave me. It was different to say the least, and I was completely enraptured by the touch that this gave me. it was like I experienced a little bit of heaven.

He pulled out, and I simply laid there on the bed, the cum inside, and the satisfaction that I felt. But then Millie moved between my legs, letting her tongue snake out, and she licked up the cum, teasing me too.

I gripped the sheets, my eyes wide with surprise, and I quickly let out a small series of cries, enjoying the feeling of this. For a moment, I was in awe at this, and I enjoyed it. I stayed like this for a bit, and then, moments later, I came hard, feeling my whole body grow ragged with pleasure.

She licked it all up, satisfied as she pulled back, looking me in the eyes with a beaming smile.

"You good there?" she asked.

"Yeah, as good as I will ever be," I told her.

"Of course. I can see that you're quite happy," she said.

"Yeah, I am," I replied.

I didn't know what else to tell her, other than I was happy, and this experience was a whole new world to me. I didn't know Millie or Jude felt this way about me, and there was something exciting about this. I wondered what this may entail, and what will come about next.

"So, what does this mean?" I asked her.

"What do you mean?" Jude asked.

"Is this like…something official? Do you guys want to do this again? I've never…had anything like this before," I told her.

She looked at me, and then she shrugged.

"Depends., you want this?" she asked me.

"I mean…only if you guys want it," I told her.

"Well, I think it would be kind of fun. What do you think Jude?" she asked.

"I would love it," Jude replied.

I flushed.

"What made you guys…want me though? I didn't expect you guys to choose me or anything," I said to them.

"We just thought you were cute, and you're a big part of our team. I figured this would be a fun way to bond together, even though it's a little different from the usual," she told me.

She did have a point. This was different, and I kind of liked it.

"Well, I don't mind different, that's for sure," I told her.

"Alright, well I'm glad that you're fine with it. We should probably get dressed though. The last thing I want is one of the security guards to come over here and try to find us," Jude said.

"Do they normally do that?"

"Oh yeah. They've almost caught us having sex in here," Millie said with a chuckle.

I flushed. These two were fucking in the room here off hours. And maybe even during work hours too. I don't know, there was something kind of exciting about that.

"Well, I wouldn't mind doing this again, and staying with both of you on the team as well. I know that we're supposed to work together but...I wouldn't mind something else too," I told them.

"We can arrange that," Jude said.

"Of course. It would be fun for all of us," Millie said with a wink.

I looked at them, realizing that they enjoyed this. This was a fun little game for both of them, and I was just a part of it these days. And yet, I didn't mind that. It was something that made me feel good, and something that I enjoyed.

And yet, I wondered what would become of us next.

We got dressed, leaving the lab and giving one another little winks and smiles. We would have to pretend that we didn't do anything, and during the day, they were forbidden. They were a happy, married couple who weren't secretly degenerates that would fuck their lab partners, but I also kind of liked it like this.

It meant that they were kind of a dirty little secret for me, something that only I could know about, and something that I enjoyed. And while I wished I could just expose the truth, and come forward with my feelings, this was the best way to do it.

And not only that, but they also showed me a whole bunch of new things and awakened new feelings within me. If nothing else, I loved that they did that period, and I couldn't wait for whatever would come our way next, and whatever it was that they had planned not just for now, but for the upcoming future that we would share as well.

Lana's Secret

Bisexual Threesomes, Hot Wives

"Bye honey, I'll see you later," I said.

"Alright, Lana. Love you," my husband Charlie said to me.

I smiled, but then as he left my face lowered. I couldn't stop thinking about her.

Amelia.

I flushed thinking about Amelia, the woman who lived next door to me. I shivered with delight thinking about her.

The truth was, I had a big crush on Amelia. She was another lonely housewife, but her husband was gone. They did have an open relationship, where she could fuck whoever she wanted, but the truth was, I did have a crush on her but was afraid to tell my husband about it.

But would Charlie get it?

Maybe, I didn't know...

We planned to meet up for lunch today, and I was making sure that I looked my best. Amelia was gorgeous, and she didn't have kids, so it made things easier.

I did, but they were older.

So I had some free time. And of course, they could take care of themselves. I knew they'd probably be out with friends based on what they told me.

Which made things even better. I got ready, putting on the nicest dress possible, doing my hair up, and looking cute. I smiled, excited about this.

I was ready to see Amelia

I went over to her place, which was only one door down. When I got there, she opened the door, seeing me.

"Hey there hun."

"Hey! How have you been?" I asked her.

I saw her smile, moving her body a little bit towards me.

"Good. And you?"

"Pretty good. Excited to eat and catch up?" she said.

"Totally," I replied.

We went over to the living room, where the sandwiches were made. As we sat there, I could feel the tension growing. She wanted to say something, but I wasn't sure what exactly.

"Something the matter?" I asked her.

She looked at me, flushing crimson.

"So, there's…something I wanted to ask you," she said.

"What is it?"

She leaned in, whispering to me.

"Wait, you're serious?"

"Yeah.... I was thinking we could have a little bit of fun like that you know? It would be good for both of us," she said to me.

I flushed, and then I nodded.

"Yeah, I wouldn't mind that. In fact, I...I kinda wanted to ask about that," I told her.

She beamed.

"Yeah, I would love that too," she told me.

I was excited. We sat there, talking about it for a bit.

"You sure it's okay? Your husband won't be mad?"

"You kidding me? We have an open relationship for a reason hun. I want this, and I can make it a ton of fun for both of us. Because I know that you want it too," she told me with a purr.

I flushed, and then nodded.

"You got me," I said.

"Come on, you and I both know that this will be fun," she said.

"Yeah, I know," I replied.

I felt excited. We devised the plan. I texted my kid to make sure she wouldn't be home. Sure enough, she told me she was going to Maddie's house and wouldn't be home till the next day.

Perfect.

We got everything ready for when Charlie decided to come home. It was a bit nerve-wracking to say the least, but I also was more than ready to see what may happen next.

That's when we put the plan into action.

We started to hang out in the bedroom together, looking at the clock. Amelia was right there near me, looking me in the eyes.

"So...have you ever done anything with a woman before?" she asked.

I shook my head.

"No, but...I kind of want to... actually more than kind of," I said.

She reached out, touching my arm and looking me in the eyes.

"Well, I'm glad that...that you want to do this," she said to me.

I looked at her, seeing the way that her eyes focused on mine.

"Yeah, I'm a little nervous about this, but I'll try to do my best," I told her.

"Don't worry, just let me take the lead," she insisted.

I wanted to believe that this was something that I enjoyed. I felt a little bit nervous about this, and I knew that this was something that she wanted just as much.

She reached out, touching my hair and looking me in the eyes. She then moved forward, our lips mere inches away from each other. I looked at this, and then, moments later, she pressed her lips to my own.

She kissed me, and for a long time, we stayed like this, enjoying the touch of one another and the feeling of this, and in truth...I kinda wanted more from her.

We stayed like this for a long time, simply moving our hands towards one another, and we made out slightly. There was a thrill that came from this.

Her lips were softer, much softer than a man's, and there was something I liked about that. She then deepened the kiss, our lips moving slightly towards one another, enjoying the pleasure of this. For a long time, she simply stayed like this with me, and we both enjoyed one another.

This was something that I wanted more than anything else, if you wanted the truth of it. I thought about having sex with Amelia beforehand. She was so damn attractive, and I'd been curious about experimentation. However, I didn't know how to...approach this until now.

But as we kissed, it awoke something within me, a new feeling that turned me the fuck on, and made me ache for more. We stayed like this, and for a long time, we simply enjoyed one another, and the feeling that this gave us.

That's what I enjoyed more than anything else. The feeling this provided, and the fun that it gave me a chance to experience.

We continued to make out for a bit, and Amelia soon moved her hands downward, touching the sides of my body, moving toward my breasts. Her hands moved there, cupping the orbs and making me shiver and tense up.

"Something the matter?" Amelia asked.

I flushed, shaking my head.

"No, it's just...this feels nice," I said.

She beamed.

"I know that it does. I take it you've never been touched by a woman before," she said.

"No, I...I haven't," I said.

I never had the balls to tell him about it, the secret that I had. I am bisexual, and I've always lusted after women, so it's hard for me to...to totally make this easy to explain. But I liked talking to Amelia about it. It made me realize that I wasn't alone and that there was someone else who liked me.

"Well don't worry, I'll be sure to show you a good time. I want to focus on you, and I'm sure that Charlie will definitely enjoy the fun that we have in store," she teased.

I hoped so too. But of course, my thoughts soon changed to that of lust as she moved her hands downward, right up against my lingerie. Was she going to take it off? A part of me hoped so, but I wasn't totally sure what her plans were for this.

She fiddled with the clasp of it, looking me in the eyes as if to ask me about it. I mean, it's not like I wanted her to stop or anything.

"Do you…want this?" she asked.

"Yes," I cried out.

I felt a sudden excitement start to flood through my body at the idea of her teasing, playing with me, touching me like this.

It brought a new sense of thrill to me, and as she moved her hands towards me, touching my curves, feeling me up, it awakened something within me.

A desire for her. A desire for so much more.

I knew Charlie would freak as soon as he got home, and I wondered what he would say. I didn't think it would be anything too bad though. He knew how I felt about…women, that's for sure, and I certainly was a bit curious about all of this, so I figured that this would be the beginning of something new, exciting, and fun as well.

As we kissed, she pushed me down on the bed, hovering over me. She touched the tip of my nipples through the top that I wore, and I let out a small gasp, holding onto her as she touched my body.

"Please," I said out loud.

"Please, what? I can't hear you there Lana," she said.

I let out a low moan, holding onto her as she did this. But of course, as soon as I uttered a sound, the door opened, and Charlie was there.

"Lana? What is this? He asked me.

I flushed, but then Amelia gave him a small smile.

"We wanted to wait for you to join us Charlie, but it seems we both...had other plans," she purred.

"But what...is this? What's going on?" he asked.

"I figured the three of us could have some fun together," I told her.

She looked at me, and for a moment, he sighed.

"Well...if you want this, I'm not going to say no to it, that's for sure," he pointed out.

"Of course, you won't say no. You want this too, don't you," she said.

"Yes," he said, his voice laced with pleasure. I knew that Charlie couldn't hold himself back either.

I smiled, and then moved towards him, giving him a long, passionate kiss.

"Don't worry, you know my husband and I are open," she said.

"Of course, and what about you Lana? Are you...okay with this?" he asked.

Of course I was. It was something that I felt deep within me, something that I enjoyed. It was like...like it was pulling me forward, and I wanted to experience more of this.

I felt a little bit shocked that this was something that I wanted though. And that it was actually happening. She leaned forward, giving me a small kiss on the lips.

"Don't worry hun. We'll take this nice and slow. Since I know that's what you like," she said.

"Yes," I said.

I wanted to feel both of them and to crave both as well. That's when I saw Charlie's eyes look into my own, pulling me there and kissing me with a passion that I hadn't experienced up till this point. Perhaps he enjoyed this as much as I did or something.

Or maybe, it was awakening something deep within him as well. As we kissed, my hands moved downward, and I felt her lips against my neck, touching me slightly with little touches. I let out a small whimper, enjoying the touch of both of them, but still lost in the feeling that this gave me, and the pleasure that I felt.

For a long time, I was completely in awe at how nice this felt, and how it made me feel...good in a sense. She then moved her hands down toward where the edge of my lingerie was. She teased the bra cup, looking up at me. Charlie pulled his lips away, his hands resting down at my waist, as I looked at Lana.

"Do you want me to continue?" she asked.

"Do you need to ask?" I told her.

She smiled, enjoying this.

"Well, I'm glad that the feeling is mutual then," she said.

"Ahh, it is," I told her.

It really was, and I liked the feeling of her hands against the very edge of my body, touching me there. She then moved towards the back of the little lingerie that I wore, unhooking the bra, pulling it off of me. I suddenly tensed up, feeling a bit surprised by everything, but also...it was nice to have this. I was just glad to experience the touch of this.

I felt Charlie's hands there too, touching and teasing my waist, while Amelia moved her lips to the tip of my nipple. She took the tip of it into her mouth, sucking on the flesh there, making me suddenly tense up, moan, and feel amazing in the process.

There was something about this whole thing that made my head spin. Her lips were like a drug, one that I couldn't get enough of, while I also noticed Charlie's hands were a lot rougher, and I liked that about them. I enjoyed the feeling of two different types of people, and of the way their hands and lips trailed against my body.

I noticed Charlie's hands move between my legs, touching my inner thighs, running his hand there until he got between my legs. As he touched me there, I let out a small gasp, surprised by how nice this felt, completely in awe at how much my body reacted to everything. It was so good, a pleasurable experience, and I certainly enjoyed this too.

For a long time, I felt like this was the beginning of a new life, a new world, and for me, I wanted to experience everything about it.

Then, I felt hands move towards my breasts, touching and cupping them. As she did that, she purred her words into my ear, making me shiver with delight.

"You have the cutest tits you know," she said.

"Really? Thanks," I said.

She giggled, letting her fingers drape against her body, and as she did this, I let out a small gasp, enjoying everything that came out of this. For a long time, I simply just laid there, enjoying the touch of her hands, and the feeling of her body.

She knew exactly how to turn me the fuck on, and I simply just enjoyed this, and I knew that she liked to hear me make delicious sounds. I felt Charlie's hands move closer and closer to the obvious heat between my legs, and it made me realize that he liked this too.

I didn't realize just how...good this felt, and as I stayed there, holding onto the bed, I felt her lips finally tease the tip of my nipples, kissing the edges, and then, her other hand moved to my other nipple, touching there slightly. When she did that, I gripped the sheets, letting out a small cry of pleasure as she continued to touch me there, the excitement, the tease, everything surrounding this making my body heavy with need.

It was rare to feel this good, but her lips were nice and soft, and they touched me perfectly, and for a brief moment, I simply closed my eyes, feeling my whole body move forward, reaching forward to touch her hair. She looked at me, smiling as she swiveled a tongue out, teasing the very tip of my nipple. As she did this, I held onto the edge of the bed, letting my moans fill the room, and the obvious enjoyment of such beginning to flow through me.

It was heavenly, it was so good, and there was something exciting about this that made me ache for her, and I knew that she liked this too. I then felt her start to move her hands against my other nipple, pinching and touching there. She smiled as I moved my hands up to her, feeling her lips deepen this, and her body start to move against my own.

"Fuck," I said.

"You're very fun to tease. I'm sure Charlie likes this. And maybe you can help him out a little bit too," she said.

I turned to Charlie, who had an obvious tent in his pants, and when he watched us, I saw the little lip-bite that he had.

"Of course. He just needs to give it to me," I told him.

"I will," Charlie said.

He moved towards the side of my body, undoing his pants, and I eagerly took out his cock. He was big and girthy, perfect for me, and I soon moved my lips to the very tip of this, enjoying the sensation that this gave to me. it was like he knew immediately what I wanted, pushing his dick right into my mouth and letting me hungrily take it there. I licked and teased the very tip of his cock, enjoying the delicious sounds that came out of this, but of course, as I did this, I noticed that Amelia's hands were moving downward, touching my taut stomach. I blushed as she got right over my panties, seeing the obvious heat that was there. She looked me in the eyes as if begging for me to agree to this.

"You ready?" she asked.

It would be the first time that I'd...do this with a woman. Sure, I've given head before, but I've never received this from the same gender. I simply nodded.

"Sure. Of course," I said, unsure of what to say, other than of course, the feeling of desire that seemed to just only drive me closer and closer to the edge. She simply nodded.

"Don't worry, we can take this nice and gentle," she said.

I watched as she spread me apart, looking me in the eyes. She grabbed each side of the waistband of my panties, sliding them off, looking me in the eyes as I nodded.

She then touched me there, feeling the obvious wetness that was there. She then beamed.

"Damn, turned on already? How hot," she said.

"Yeah," I said, suddenly unable to breathe. I took Charlie's cock in my mouth once more, letting my lips move against it, touching and pleasuring him. I wanted him, but I also wanted to see what Amelia would do.

What I didn't know, was that Amelia knew exactly where to go with her hands. the first thing that she did was run her fingers against the very edge of my pussy, the little touch enough to set me on fire. I watched her move her hands towards my clit, barely rubbing there, and for a long time, I simply just stayed there, completely lost in the touch. I felt the cock slide in and out of my mouth, and I was completely enraptured by the feeling of pleasure that came out of this. I started to move my hands towards his cock, taking the second half there, jerking it while I sucked and teased the other part of the tip with my lips. I felt good, and with every single touch, I could sense that there was something about this that turned me into something more, something needy, and I loved everything about it.

I eagerly sucked on his cock, but then I felt the finger rub up against the very tip of my clit, touching there. I let out a small, garbled moan, enjoying the feeling of this. I watched as he simply smiled, pushing it further down my throat. I felt a bit of a gag as he did this, but that didn't matter.

What did matter, was what Amelia was doing between my legs.

She let her fingers dance there, teasing every part of me. I suddenly felt her fingers slowly move downward, touching the very tip of my entrance, then moving against there again. She rubbed my clit a few times, repeating the motions, but then, as she did this, she moved her tongue outward, touching the very tip of my clit, licking and teasing the very edge of it, making me suddenly lose control. I held onto her, and then I let out a moan around his cock, feeling him let out a small groan of desire and approval as he heard me continue to get overtaken by everything that's going on here. I then watched as he moved his hands to the sides of my head, fucking my throat, but then, as he did that, it was like a signal to Amelia, and then, she moved her tongue there, letting it circle against my clit, causing me to let out a small series of moans and grunts.

I didn't expect this to feel that good, but here I was, completely reduced to nothing as I held onto her, whimpering with pleasure as I felt her move her lips around, and I looked at her, seeing how she was between my legs, buried there. I looked at her, seeing that she didn't want to stop. She then pushed her tongue in, letting it explore me, and it was then when she angled herself a bit, and her tongue touched a part of me that made me suddenly cry out, holding onto the very edge of the sheets, letting out a cry against Charlie's cock as I felt my orgasm right there.

But then, she pulled away, smiling towards me.

"I don't think you want to cum just yet," she said.

"No," I said, admitting that I was trying to hold back.

By this point, I needed something inside of me right now, whether it be him or her, and when I looked at Charlie, I saw the smile that he had.

"You ready?" he asked me.

"Born…ready," I told him.

Charlie gave me a nod of approval, pushing me down so that I was on my hands and knees, but instead of doing that, I shook my head.

"I think maybe…I should get on top," I told him.

"You sure about this?" he asked me.

"Yeah," I told him.

He looked at me, nodding in agreement, and then got on the bed. I quickly got on top, moving myself so that I was right over his cock. As I slid down on him, I felt the familiar sensation, but then, I looked over at her, surprised by the little smile of excitement that she gave me.

"You good?" she asked me.

"Yes, I am," I told her.

She beamed, and then took off her panties, sliding her wet, shaven pussy over my husband's face. She let out a small cry as he started to explore her with his tongue, touching, teasing, and playing with her folds.

Meanwhile, I began pushing my hips up, holding onto the bed for a moment. As I did this, I looked over, and she simply smiled.

"Fuck...Charlie is good," she said.

"He is. He's good at what he does," I said.

"Indeed. But I think I'm a little bit better," she told me.

I flushed and then smiled.

"That's something I'm not going to debate you on," I told her.

"Yeah," she replied.

She then moved herself away and started to ride him. I did the same. Both of us let out small moans of excitement and need, the pleasure obvious between our bodies. She looked me in the eyes, reaching out and touching my face. As she did so, she reached in, pressing her lips to my own. I kissed her passionately, feeling her hips move about, and there was something exciting about all of this.

I knew for a fact that she was enjoying this as much as I was, and soon, I noticed that Charlie's lips were teasing her. After a few more moments, she leaned in, giving me a passionate kiss, rubbing between my legs as she did. Moments later, I tensed up, holding onto her, letting out a small cry of surprise as I suddenly felt the urge to cum hard.

When I finally did, I laid back, feeling my whole body just relax right then and there. I looked at her, and then, she smiled.

"You good?" she said.

"Yeah but...what about you? You still need to cum. And so does Charlie?" I told her.

She looked at Charlie, who smiled.

"Want to take me for a test ride?" she asked.

"I thought you'd never ask," he replied.

She got down on her hands and knees, sticking her thick ass upward, and then, he grabbed it, pushing himself deep into her. She let out a small cry of surprise and pleasure, holding onto the very edge of the bed as she did this. She looked at me, giving me a small smile of excitement.

"There we go," she said.

"You good?" I asked her.

"Better than good babe," she said.

She then spread my legs once more, diving right in, letting her lips and tongue move and tease against me. As she did that, she let out a series of small cries against my pussy, letting her tongue loll over me. I noticed Charlie holding onto her hips, thrusting in deep, filling her up.

Honestly seeing them together was hot as fuck, and then, I felt her lips move towards my clit, licking and sucking on it, while two fingers moved into me, pleasuring me.

As she did that, I let out a small cry, holding onto her, and then, moments later, I could feel the throes of my orgasm start to wash over me once again. But she stopped it for a second, looking at me.

"I'm...close too," she said.

I could tell that Charlie was too. Then, after a few more thrusts, he reached down, touching between her legs, and then, she let out a small moan of surprise, and seconds later, Charlie groaned, spilling himself into her.

She pressed her fingers against that little spot once again, and then, as she did that, I started to let out a small gasp, enjoying the feeling. It was then when I came hard, feeling like I was suddenly lost in the feeling of this. Completely shocked by how good...it felt. It was amazing, totally different from what I expected, and then, moments later, I finished too.

We laid there, all of us looking at one another. There was clearly something more that we wanted to say, but then, I felt Amelia reach over, giving me a small kiss on the lips.

"You good?" she asked me.

"Amazing really," I told her.

"I'm glad. I knew that you'd enjoy this. Because I sure as shit did," she said.

I wasn't going to lie, I felt the same way too. But what did this mean for us? What now? I could sense that Charlie was curious too.

"Well...I had a good time with this, even though it was quite surprising to see you in that state there babe," he said.

"Yeah sorry, it was a plan that we had," I told him.

"Well, next time give me a bit of a heads up before you do that," he said.

"Aww but it was a surprise," I heard Amelia say.

"Well, we can hint at it a little bit better I guess," I told her with a small smile.

"Indeed. God that was fun. I haven't had a lay that good in a long time. You would think it'd be easy to find someone, but nope," she said.

"Sounds like it," I told her.

"Anyways, enough about me, so what do you guys say? want to do it again?" Amelia asked us.

I flushed, and in truth, I wanted to. But when I looked over at Charlie, I could see something else.

The flames of desire. He wanted this too.

"You sure about that?"

"Yes, I'm sure," she told me.

"Well, then I guess we can arrange something like that. I for one had a great time and well...it was nice doing this with you, Amelia," he said.

"Indeed. Anyways, I should probably get going. We can talk again later Lana," she said.

As she walked away, closing the door, I felt the awkward tension between Charlie and I, then Charlie sighed. "Next time you do this, can you at least let me know what's going on," he said.

"Sorry, it was a decision on a whim. But you seemed to enjoy this, right?" I told him.

"Yes of course. I enjoyed it," he told me.

I blushed, and then, moments later he leaned in, capturing my lips with his own. We made out for a bit, and I did enjoy this. Even though he was definitely my one and only, having a little bit of fun with Amelia was a good thing too.

"But next time warn a guy. Coming home to that was something to say the least," he teased.

"Sure was," I told him.

"But I'd be lying if I said I didn't enjoy this," he said to me.

I flushed, and there was something about the way that he looked at me that I enjoyed. I certainly had a wonderful time with him, and it showed me...something new about myself. There was clearly a desire there, something that excited me, and something that I was enjoying too.

For a long time, the two of us spent time just making out and having a good time together, both of us enjoying the touch of one another. While I did have fun with her, I was happy to be back with him, the guy that I loved and adored.

But I was also kind of glad that...my secret was finally revealed. That's what was so exciting about all of this. The fact that I was enjoying this, and the way that he seemed to like this, it was all simply magical, and very fun too. I certainly liked it, and I knew that he did as well.

But I did wonder what would happen next, or even what the future may hold. I also kind of wondered what Amelia thought about this, if she really wanted to do this again or not. I assumed so, but who knows.

There is one thing that I knew for sure, and that was the fact that I knew that it was the beginning of an exciting arrangement. Her husband wouldn't be back for a little bit, so that would give us a lot of time to play around, to explore one another more, and to let me indulge in the secret fun that I wanted to have as well.

www.ingramcontent.com/pod-product-compliance
Lightning Source LLC
Chambersburg PA
CBHW032004180726
48283CB00008B/2558